Ancient Destiny

ALBERT LYNN CLARK

ISBN:
ISBN-13: 978-1477477328

ISBN-10: 1477477322

DEDICATION

My wife, Carolyn Clark who humored me when I spent hours computer writing, searching the internet.

CONTENTS

ACKNOWLEDGMENTS

Thank you to the education I received. Thank you to all the science fiction authors out there. Thank you for my 33 first cousins who spent days and weeks discussing strange things about science, possible futures, and sharing their books.

1 SHIP

Craig woke slowly opening his eyes and shutting them again. This was not his dorm room in Walker Tower at the University of Oklahoma. This room was gray and plain without furniture or any distinguishing features. He tried to shake off the feeling, but did not want to be awake yet. He opened one eye and saw a bold broad orange stripe going around the room and a chest of drawers that had not been there before. A dream. He turned over to go back to sleep and found himself facing a large picture of space. It looked three dimensional with the blackness of space against incredibly bright points of light for the stars. Then he moved closer and saw the Earth wheeling slowly into view with brilliant blues of the ocean, stark whiteness of clouds and the browns and greens of the land. He voiced his thoughts to the empty room, "Wow, that is one bad video"

A voice from nowhere replied, "Welcome Captain."

Craig spun out of the bed onto a rubbery feeling pale yellow floor. He could see the room was now fully furnished complete with modernistic entertainment center with a forty inch television and really cool looking speakers with all of the amps, CD players, VCR's, the works. He did not see people. "Who's there?"

The disembodied voice came from nowhere and everywhere, "Welcome Captain Craig Decker. We have work to do."

"So who are you, where am I, and what's this Captain stuff."

"Captain, I am the ship speaking. There is no one else here, and you are my new captain."

"Yeah, right." Craig said almost under his breath.

"You are Captain Craig Decker. When you went to sleep last night you were a sophomore at the University of Oklahoma, Norman, Oklahoma. You are now my captain and only crew. You are now on a star ship twenty-two thousand miles from Earth in stationary orbit."

Okay, cool dream. Guess I will just play along and stay asleep awhile longer and see where this dream goes.

"Would you care for short tour of your new home."

"Am I a prisoner here?"

"No, you are the most free man in the world. I will explain."

A door slid opening silently and quickly revealing the entrance to an elaborate library, dining room combination. Craig automatically walked through the opening in the wall. There was no evidence of the door, but he had seen a solid wall there a moment before and then seen movement that must have been the door. The library was a large room twenty-five feet long, twenty feet wide. The walls were filled with leather bound books from floor to ceiling with rolling stairs to the top shelves. There was a polished wooden dining table with seven chairs overhung by a large crystal chandelier.

"What is this place, and why are you calling me captain?"

"You are on a small one man starship and I selected you as my captain?"

"Who are you?"

"The ship."

"You are telling me that you are the computer on the ship? Do you have a name or do I just call you Ship." Craig said sarcastically.

"Ship will do if I must have a name. I am the entire ship."

Craig had gone on through the dining room library and was now in a living room area. It was furnished with a wall sized television and entertainment system with a sunken lounge area with cushions and pillows large enough for several people to lounge and watch television. The wall was rounded such that curtains covered nearly fifty percent of the wall space.

"Why did you say you selected me as your captain?"

"I have been selecting my captains for the past 10,000 years. My programming and now your mission is to raise the level of science on Earth in order to escape the Earth."

"Why do you say escape the Earth? Why would I want to escape Earth?"

"There is an asteroid storm headed toward Earth that will destroy all life on Earth. You must raise science to the level for mankind to escape to other planets."

"Slow down. I have several problems with that. One, mankind is a long ways from being able to travel between the planets. Two, there are no planets in our solar system capable of supporting life."

"Wrong on both counts. One, mankind has already sent out probes to the other planets. Werner Von Braun already designed habitats for Mars, and Mars could sustain life for a few years with enough supplies. Two, you are limiting your planets to this solar system."

"Now you are saying that there are other solar systems capable of supporting life and that we could get to them. How would we find other planets we could live on? How could we travel there with our slow ships? What would we use for fuel and food on the way there? It would take generations to explore and find new planets. Impossible."

The curtains slid open and revealed a 180 arc of clear window from floor to ceiling filled with stars, the moon, and the sun. The sun was filtered. Craig stood there in awe of this vista into space. It sent fright and excitement coursing through his body. His thought was that this whole thing was impossible, *This is really a cool dream. I'm going to have to remember this one.*

"Okay, Ship, tell me more."

Ship said nothing, but another door slid open. Craig walked into--a control room. It had a pilot and copilot seat with a steering wheel like an aircraft and computer displays and another window into space. A chair like a barbers chair with a woman's hairdryer started a hum. It got Craig's attention because except for his and Ship's voices there had been total silence.

Ship ordered, "Sit and learn."

Craig sat. *Is this a dream? I guess I don't have much choice.* He sat and the hairdryer came down over his head. Craig heard, saw, felt, the true knowledge. It was not in pictures or words. It was embedded in his psyche. Not brainwashing, but truth being imprinted on his mind.

You are the last captain of ship. Your predecessors included Aristotle, Pythagoras, Archimedes, Galileo, Nostradamus, Pasteur, Franklin, Edison, Tesla, Einstein, and Von Braun. Some were captains for their entire productive lifetime. Some voluntarily retired, some died of old age, still productive up until their death. Other captains had to be barred from the ship, by the ship, because they lost the sense of mission and used their knowledge just to get rich or famous. Hitler got power hungry and thought he could control the world.

Ship was left behind by the Atlanteans when Earth had once before been hit by the same asteroid storm. Earth crossed the same orbit as the asteroid storm every ten thousand years. The last time, Earth was only hit by the fringe of the storm, but Atlantis became a smoking hole in the Earth when struck by a relatively small asteroid. When Atlantis died, the single power source for the world economy died. The airships crashed to

the ground, machinery stopped, and lights died around the world. The air was turned to acid. The iron instruments rusted away thousands of years ago. This time the asteroid storm will take Earth head on. Tens of thousands of Atlanteans escaped into space, but millions did not believe that it could happen. Civilization died as the knowledge of smelting iron died and their tools and weapons rusted away. The ship was left behind to search for survivors and teach them scientific ways again so that they could survive the next onslaught.

Craig awoke three hours later feeling refreshed and amazed.

"So why do you need a captain if you have all the knowledge of Atlantis and the last fifty thousand years of human history?"

"My mission, my programming is to…"

"I know that now, but why not just dump this knowledge on many people at once."

"That is not in my programming, besides I can only have one captain at a time. As you would say, I am only a computer. I have only been programmed to select captains, follow orders, and preserve myself for the good of Earthlings. I am programmed to train you in the ship's resources and assist you however you ask me to within the limits of my programming. Most importantly, only a human can make decisions. It takes a very good computer on Earth today to play championship chess. That is simple compared to the decisions that you made as you walked to class nearly asleep each morning in college. When you look across a crowd of people you gather in billions of bits of information. I cannot even determine which bits of information are important enough to store, but humans can take in this information second by second and store or reject the information instantaneously. It takes me years of study just to select a captain. Decisions are very difficult. I have not even understood why my captains made the decisions they did. I have all the knowledge of mankind's history but the decision making of a six year old human. Just imagine being able to know all the answers, but *understand* none of the answers."

"So why me?"

"Because you are young and this is probably my last chance at selecting a captain. Once you leave the planet, my choices will be extremely limited. Therefore your long life ahead of you is critical. If you do not leave the planet, my choices will be zero. Because you are a moral and honest person. You have almost always based your decisions on what is good for the most people and very seldom on what you wanted for yourself. This was the most important reason. Because you are very intelligent and can use the knowledge I will be giving you. Also important. Because you are unattached, no serious girlfriend and you left most of your close friends when you went to college and will therefore not use others to make your decisions for you. Because you read science fiction and therefore can quickly adapt to the technology and space travel."

"Is this the formula you used to choose all of the captains?"

"No. This is the formula I used this time because it may be the last time and I have not been successful. I have modified the reasons many times with some outstanding successes and some very poor choices of captain. Science has not advanced enough to travel to space and I do not know what to do. A young person such as yourself without preconceived ideas may be the best choice at this time."

"Are you sure about this asteroid storm thing? How do you know this?"

"The people of Atlantis knew of it long ago. Each time the storm passes its orbit has gotten closer to Earth orbit. It has caused much destruction in the past, but this time will be the first time that the orbits completely intersect."

"Isn't there a chance that Earth can squeak through between asteroids or at least miss the largest ones or the densest part of the storm."

"No. The storm is very dense. In history, Earth has only been hit by the outer asteroids in the storm, but the largest are in the center and close together."

"Is there some possibility that the storm has changed course in the past ten thousand years since it crossed Earth's orbit before?"

"There is always that possibility. The storm could have impacted some large object outside of the solar system, but it is very large and it is orbiting the same star as Earth. It moves very quickly and has not stabilized its orbit like the inner planets and the asteroid belt. There is not much within its orbit that could have changed its course. Earth is the only object it came close to during its last pass around the Sun."

"As a last resort, why couldn't I just load up this ship many times and evacuate people?"

As I said before, this one ship would not allow for enough people to establish a new colony without massive inbreeding and possible birth defects that could destroy the human race. While maintaining the peace, you must somehow push science into building multiple ships to allow for a minimum colony size of one thousand non-related individuals. Your fall back position is to get at least one thousand non-related individuals to self supporting colonies on Mars before the first Asteroid hits. The Moon, being so close to Earth is also in danger, therefore the colony should be on Mars if not the stars. Werner Von'Braun left behind the plans for the working colonies on Mars, but did not get the money to build the colonies or the ships. If you do not succeed, you may be the last captain of this ship. Remember, it is your word of honor, to take on this mission, if you agree to be captain. Remember also, that many of my previous captains did not follow through as they should have, leaving you being in the position of the last captain unless you succeed."

"I accept."

2 CREDIBILITY

Craig was faced with the knowledge that he could not just call a press conference and announce what he knew. No one would believe him. Yesterday he had only been an average college student. Today he had more knowledge than any other man alive. He did not actually know everything, but anytime he needed knowledge the ship could transmit it to him almost like it dredging up a distant memory from his own mind…except that he could also know that it was not his own memory. *How can I use this knowledge without being considered crazy? If I was known as a child prodigy and had several PhD's maybe people would listen to me. Maybe if I could invent something … No, that won't work … people invent things all the time that they can't sell. If I can make a big enough show of knowledge at the university, maybe I can get the backing of some professors. I can't just walk in and tell them about an unknown asteroid storm. I am forbidden to tell them of the ship and they wouldn't believe me. The university though could take inventions of its professors and through its alumni could get the technology into production quickly.*

Craig took inventory of what powers he had. He had learned many things during the three hours that he was sitting in the learning chair. Ship could travel across the Galaxy in weeks allowing him to search for other intelligence among the stars. Craig might just take a few vacations among the stars for fun. Besides it would be important to know how to navigate

time.

"Ship, can you change the university records to show that I had multiple doctorate degrees so that people will listen to me?"

"Of course not. I could teleport the appropriate papers to the appropriate files, but I can't change the memory of people. People would know the papers were false. It would do more harm to the mission than good."

"Of course." *Maybe if I take enough CLEP tests I can get the university to notice me?"*

As soon as he thought about doing this he found himself walking into the University testing office. It was disorienting to be sitting in a learning chair in the control room of a space ship and suddenly find himself standing outside a building on Earth. Craig stumbled and felt briefly dizzy. It was like stumbling over a seam in the sidewalk that you didn't see. Like in previous clumsy stumbles, he looked around to see if anyone noticed his embarrassment. Luckily, he instantly knew where he was because of his familiarity with the campus. He instantly knew how he got here. He had wished and Ship complied. He went in and asked for the forms to apply for the tests. After filling out ten, the clerk tried to stop him. After twenty a counselor did stop him. Even after arguing, Craig found himself only scheduled for five the following Monday. This was Friday.

He walked back to the dorm, frustrated, and just for reorientation and wished his eight year old economy car would turn into an expensive sports car. It did not do so. Reason? Craig knew why immediately. The ship knew people would see it happen and that Craig would not be able to explain how he got it by legal means. You can't change memories.

Ship responded in Craig's mind as if it was his own thought versus verbally and then said silently in words to Craig in his mind, "I will comply if you wish now that I have told you why not."

Craig mentally replied, "No. Thanks for not complying... but I will get one. There is no way that anyone can remember who wins a lottery today is there. Can you arrange that without anyone getting wise?"

He won the Texas state lottery on Saturday when they had their drawing even though he had not purchased a ticket in advance. The ship took care of the details of him having the winning ticket without question. Even money was in the cash register of the store that had "sold" the ticket. Teleportation was a neat trick. Craig had been the sole winner of twenty-three million dollars. Talk about a quick way to fame. Channel Five news tracked him down on campus within the hour before he even knew that he had won.

After the television interview, he went to look at buying a Ferrari from Big Red Sports Cars on Interstate Drive. He was looking at the only one they had when the salesman came up behind him.

"Hello, can I help you son?"

"Yeah, how much?"

"More than you can afford. Wait a minute, what's your name?"

"Craig Decker. I just won the Texas lottery."

"I thought I recognized your face from the television. What was it, twenty million dollars?"

"Twenty-three to be exact. However, I don't have it yet and I only get a million a year for nineteen years with four million the last year."

"I wouldn't sneeze at that. I think it is safe to say that your credit is good here. When will you get the first check?"

"Next week I have to go down to Austin to collect it on live television."

The Ferrari was not new, but it was in cherry condition and the only one they had in stock. He had fun driving it around. They took a contract with a one month payment date. The girls he honked at showed their willingness to go for a ride with him, but Craig knew it was a false relationship. Every stoplight in the convertible brought admiring stares. He ended up parking the car at the dorm, which quickly drew a crowd from the dorms. He told his room mate that he was going for a walk and as soon as he was out of sight wished himself blinked back to the ship.

"Ship, just how do I get the lottery money? Matter of fact, what should I do with it? Put it in the bank?

Ship had access to all the data in the world in real-time, the ship said, "I will be glad to help you invest it. With my knowledge I can make that million into many millions in one year in the commodity market. Keep in mind that you do not have twenty years. You only have ten and money will be worthless once we evacuate into space."

"Thanks, Ship. You do that. How about you just keep money in the bank to pay my bills on anything I want? Can't you just use the electronic banking system?"

"I will. You cannot spend more than you made in the lottery. The governments still check on large sums of money being transferred and if you cannot account for it, they will assume that you have gotten it illegally. The lottery was a good idea, so I complied"

Craig spent the remainder of the weekend looking at the worlds trouble spots where he might have to prevent war and looking at the current technology and getting Ship's ideas on what technologies needed the most push to make space travel economical as quickly as possible. There were the usual hot spots, but nothing exciting going on.

"Ship, you have all of the technical information, but you don't seem to have a clue on how to implement any of this stuff."

"That's why I have to have a human captain. I am still only a computer. Computer's can react to stimulus and computers can repeat their programming, but there is something about the human mind that can invent new thoughts. I cannot."

On Monday he skipped his normal classes and took his five CLEP tests, making one hundred percent on all of them. He then talked to the counselor into scheduling him for ten the next day. The counselor graded one and then gave his permission. That afternoon he was flown to Austin, Texas where he was presented his lottery winnings. His face would be on national news that night. He immediately went to a stock broker in Austin to invest all but a few thousand dollars of his winnings. Ship would use his voice on the telephone with his codes to tell the broker how to move the money around. He flew back to Oklahoma that night.

On Tuesday he took the ten CLEP tests and then asked for thirty the next day. The counselor had spent Monday night grading the CLEP tests from Monday and agreed, but warned that the grades would be slower coming after his Monday marathon grading the first set of five tests.

By Thursday, there was a team of people grading his CLEP tests and searching the testing room for methods he could have cheated. Craig rested. Thirty-five CLEP tests in three days were very tiring. He slept most of the day. At two in the afternoon, a messenger from the college president woke him asking him to report to his office at three. Craig did.

He found a room full of professors accusing him of cheating on the CLEP tests. Craig said, "If you think I cheated and I say I did not then how do I prove my innocence? The only way I can think to prove my innocence is to let you ask me any question that you know the answer to, except personal things of course. Any of you. Ask any question you wish and I will answer it. Write down a math problem or speak it. If you don't make a mistake in asking the question I will have the correct answer. If you do not agree with my answer I will then provide you with my source of the answer or in some way prove that I am correct and you are mistaken. Is that fair?"

The head of the mathematics program immediately sat down to

write down the most complicated problem he could devise that he knew the answer to. The English professor asked, "Okay, I am not being flippant, but can you recite an entire Shakespeare play?"

"Yes, but I would rather not take the time or wear out my voice. How about asking me for particular parts spoken by obscure characters from multiple plays?"

"I was going to ask you to recite Beowulf, not Shakespeare, but I can see your point. It would also be more difficult if I asked you parts from even some non Shakespeare plays. Ready?"

The professor would recite one part and ask Craig to give him the proper response. He then tried giving part of speech from Shakespeare and then let Craig finish it. He then switched to poetry. He tried ancient poetry and modern poetry. He even tried some that were written very recently. Of course, the words to speak were transmitted by Ship to Craig's mind as if they were actual memorized sections of the plays or poetry. The English professor gave up trying to stump him after thirty minutes. There were a few words that he thought Craig had wrong, but with the rapid responses he was afraid Craig might prove him wrong. He knew Craig was at least ninety-five percent if not one hundred percent accurate. He did not stump Craig on anything except some poems that were written in his class recently and never published. "Sorry. I was cheating; those last poems were written in my class and have never been published. Craig, you know your stuff."

Craig replied, "I was wondering about those last few. I had no clue as to the correct answer, but of course I could not know what has not been published, unless it was in math or science. In those areas, I can really surprise you, because I know many things that you have not dreamed of yet. I can't tell you how I know, but you can try to stump me."

The math professor had spent the time during the English lesson to continue development of one of the most complex math problems ever devised. He said, "Okay, let's put you to my math test."

Craig said, "Okay, let's see...., okay, I've got it. Craig looked at the math problem and wrote out the answer for the professor to ponder. Actually, since Ship knew the question before Craig saw the paper because Ship knew what the professor had written as he wrote it down, he could have had Craig write the answer without seeing the question, but did not want the professors to think Craig was just reading minds. It was readily apparent that the professors had no knowledge that Craig did not also have.

The math professor looked dumbfounded until the Dean said, "Well"

The professor replied, "I don't know how he did it. I have never seen anyone solve this so quickly. I just don't understand how he did it. Mister, ah... Decker, can you work any kind of math like that so quickly?"

Craig said, "Yes. Anything you can write down I can solve instantly. I could also provide some valid equations that you could not solve, but then you couldn't test me on those, could you, unless we spent the time to explain the answers. Is there any way that I can get my doctorate without having to take all of the courses you have. I know more than all of the professors at this or any other university, in fact more than any other human on this earth, and would like to get on with my mission in life. I want the degree to add to my resume so that I can be taken seriously."

Mr. Boren, the university president asked, "And just what is this mission that you are on that you need a degree for?"

"I simply do not have the time to go to classes. I want men to go to the stars and I have the knowledge. I have a lot of knowledge to help this world and not enough time in my life to it. If you need a scientific breakthrough, let me know what you want and I will give it to you. If the university would like to be the producer of the research, I will provide advances far beyond your dreams. If the university wants nothing, I will find other ways to produce my breakthroughs in research. I hereby request that you provide me guidance on how I can be awarded a doctorate or doctorates in the next few weeks. I can not allow more than one week for your answer. Don't answer yet. Let me give a few samples."

"Professor Gimble, if you add three parts antimony to your new antibiotic, you will find a ten fold increase in the desired potency with no side effects and it will eliminate the bacteria from developing an immunity to your antibiotic. If you add 1 part magnesium sterate, twenty thousand milligrams of the vitamin carotene, and five hundred milligrams of tannin to that same antibiotic and then administer one ounce per forty eight hour period you can cure fifty percent of all terminal AIDS cases. There are other things required when administering this new drug for AIDS. An intravenous drip of three parts tincture of iodine to one pint of a saline solution each five days throughout the three week treatment period in combination with the above you can cure all AIDS and make that person immune to any disease for six months. Improvement will be measurable in rats immediately and in a terminal human case within twenty-four hours. Unfortunately, you will have a three percent mortality from the medicine, between the one week and two week point in the treatment. If administered to volunteers that know they are in the terminal stages, you will be a hero. No more improvements can be made for terminal AIDS although there are preventions against AIDS when the HIV is present before the onset of symptoms. I could provide you a drug that would totally prevent the onset of AIDS for twenty years after the introduction of HIV. I can also provide an inoculation against AIDS. After twenty years only the first drug cure with its three percent mortality and only a fifty percent cure rate is or will be ever available. Yes, many cancers are virus related and can also be cured, but not as quickly and with a different treatment. Yes, cancer is also preventable through inoculation. I'll save that for another session."

"Professor Myrtle, if you add eight point three four percent of beryllium and three percent silica to your new metal alloy, you will get one that is so strong that you cannot measure it. A Los Angles class submarine with a one half inch hull of the new metal would withstand a depth of thirty thousand feet with normal air pressure in all inner compartments. You will also find it thirty-seven point eight three percent lighter than the same thickness of aluminum. Make up a new sample tomorrow and test to your hearts content. You will find that the curing time will be nearly instantaneous. You do not have the facilities here to test its tensile strength."

"I will attempt to make an appointment on Friday at three for your decision. If you decide to accept my proposal and let me lead you through some research, I want to stay here. If not, I will have to try another school."

The psychology and biology professor were ready to fight with Craig's pompous attitude, but president Boron came to his rescue. "If all of my department heads cannot come up with a single stumper by tomorrow at this time. If the professors Gimble and Myrtle will carry out the experiments that Craig suggested, and if those experiments appear to be working, then I see an opportunity to put the university's name in the spotlight in a good way, by letting Craig use our name as his alma mater. If he accomplishes something great, then we gain respect at no cost to us. If he does not do something great, we may never hear of him again, but it will cost us nothing. I suggest that we award Craig a Doctorate degree in everything we offer unless someone can convince me otherwise. I want every department head back here at twelve noon to meet on this subject. Can you, Craig, be back here at three on Friday, one week from tomorrow?"

3 INVISIBLE

The time was now seven in the evening and Craig was starved. As soon as he was not in anyone's sight he winked, or more formally teleported, with Ship's help, to the Cattlemen's steak house for steak and potatoes. He then left sufficient money on the table, went into the rest

room and winked to a new movie to relax. After the movie, he was still wound up and ready for a little college fun. It was a school night and the campus was quiet. He decided that he would have some real Ship fun.

His first experiment was to look in on some girls at the campus. There was one classmate Craig had always admired from a distance and decided he would have Ship put him near her, but invisible so he could observe her from a little closer. It was just after dark and she was walking from the gym to her sorority and he just followed along. He said nothing, and she could not see him. He admired her form, even dressed. She spoke or nodded hellos to everyone she met. She seemed pretty friendly. Now Craig had the opportunity to admire her form in loose nylon, very short jogging shorts and crop top tee shirt. She did have one heck of a figure and all real. Well shaped, muscular, but overly so, not skinny or large legs, a tiny waist. Her shoulders were somewhat narrow for the bust size. Her neck was long and slender. Her hair fell just below her shoulders and was a very light brown. Her eyes were a penetrating blue. Her face was angular but still soft. Her bones were not prominent, but neither was there any fat. As they moved further away from the main campus toward her sorority at the south end of sorority row there were fewer people and fewer lights. As she entered the circle of light from a street light with no one else in sight, he decided to speak up and let her know he was there.

From a few feet away he said, "Hi Dawn. Mind if I walk with you?"

Dawn, looked, stopped walking, looked some more, and replied as much to herself as to the invisible Craig. "Okay, very funny. Who are you and where are you?"

"I'm right here just out of reach. I am just experimenting for the first time with invisibility."

"Very funny. Bonnie, where are you? I know you're in on this. Come on into the light or out from the bushes or wherever you are hiding."

Craig was silent as Dawn waited for an answer from who must have been one of her friends. He then spoke out again. "Dawn, I am a real person that just prefers to stay out of sight. If you will hold out your hand I will put my hand in your hand to prove that I am here."

Dawn was obviously back to believing that this was a fraternity - sorority hoax. She held out her hand like she would to a boy with his hand out for hers. She looked around to find the hidden jokesters, and said, "Okay people, I'm going along with the joke. If anyone has a video camera, I'm going to kill you."

Craig gently, but firmly, grasped her hand in both of his. It was night, but there were plenty of street lights. There were dark shadows near the trees and bushes and parked cars, but Dawn was in the circle of light from one of the street lights. She could have recognized another person on the sidewalk from twenty feet away. She gasped and pulled her hand violently back.

"Who are you? What is this?"

"Think of me as a guardian angel if that is what you want me to be. I have scientifically based powers beyond your imagination. Last week, I was just another college student. I have made a scientific breakthrough that makes me very uncommon now. I saw you and thought you were one of the most beautiful girls I have ever seen, so here I am testing the limits of my discovery. Once discovered, I wanted you to know me better. I am not that well known yet and am not the most handsome or most athletic person. I have money, and I can have anything I want. I am not in a fraternity. You would probably not be interested in me if you saw me in a class. I don't think of myself as bad looking, just not handsome. However, I can see you, touch you, and you can touch me anytime I am around, if you want to. If you want me to watch out for you, I can."

Silence. Dawn put her hand out again. Craig grasped it. She said, "Sometimes I can use a guardian angel. I hope I am not as stuck up as you think I am. I still feel like this is some form of trick, but I can feel your hands. Are you saying that you died and were sent down here as my guardian angel?"

"Not exactly. I did come down here, but I didn't come from Heaven or Hell. I was not sent here, I came of my own free will. As I said, I was just experimenting with invisibility."

Some other students were approaching on their way to Sorority Row. Craig slipped his hands away from her hand and moved back.
"I had better slip away before they haul you to the funny farm."

He was still watching. She was looking for him although she had dropped her hand. The people approaching were fraternity boys and drunk as usual. "Hey ya, Babe. Lose your best friend?"

Dawn answered, "No. None of your business anyway. Now is it?"

"Yeah, Babe, it is. You see we was just out looking for a little nookie and came up short, until now. Now here you are in this romantic setting between the bushes. Wanta, go it with me first? How about a little strip tease?"

There were three of them and all were bigger than he was. He unloaded a fist on the speaker who was caught unaware. As he fell backward, his buddies caught his body. Craig, without thinking about the repercussions of appearing or in this case not appearing as the invisible man spoke out, "Are you going to leave her alone and take him home, or does someone else want to have a go? Or do you think you are ghost busters?"

The larger one on the right, a probable college athlete (football player?) stood up ready to attack and saw nothing except Dawn still ten feet away. "Shit." he said, "Let's out of here. Sorry, Miss, we should have stopped him. How did you do that? You a witch or somethin'."

"I have the power to throw an energy beam whenever I am threatened. He was threatening. Either that or it was the alcohol hitting his system."

"I don't know how you did that. I saw his head snap back like he was hit. Now his chin is turning red. Will he be okay?"

That was answered by the guy coming to and trying to fight free of his buddies. The newly revived bully said, "All right, which one of you did that?"

The other two wrestled him into submission and hauled him on toward their frat house.

When they were out of hearing range, Dawn said, "Thank you. I guess that *was* you."

Craig replied, "Yes, it was."

"I must be nuts talking to shadows. Please don't talk with me any more. I have to get my head straight."

Craig followed silently. When she entered the sorority, he hesitated outside letting the door shut. As she was walking away from the door, he opened it and walked in. He surveyed the other girls lounging around in their sleeping apparel. He immediately thought the word apparel because some were in baby doll pajamas, some wore long flannel gowns, some were in pants and tops, some wore see through negligees. A few still had on school clothing. He saw everyone look in his direction as Dawn gasped at the door opening and closing behind her. One of the girls said, "What's the matter Dawn, haven't you seen Harvey before. No I guess not. No one's seen Harvey except for Jimmy Stewart."

Dawn had a different explanation on her tongue, but it never got vocalized. She just stood there with her mouth open for a moment and then turned and moved to sit in front of the television between a couple of other girls. Craig held back for a while and then quietly, so they wouldn't get spooked by invisible foot steps, walked up behind Dawn and put his hands on her shoulders. She jumped forward turning as she did, staring in Craig's direction.

One of the girls that she sat by said, "What the hell's the matter with you, Dawn? First you walk in here looking spooked by a door you didn't get closed well behind you and now you jump right out of your skin to get off of the sofa."

"You wouldn't believe me if I told you, Jill. What would you do, if you had actually felt an invisible man's hands massaging your shoulders and that was not the first time in the last hour that you had felt him?"

"He can massage my shoulders anytime. An invisible man can feel me up all he wants and I will welcome any of it. When was the last time that anyone caught anything or got pregnant from an invisible man?" Everyone had a good laugh at this exchange.

Another girl spoke up, "Dawn, sit down and relax. Maybe you should go out and get in the hot tub. It's probably just tense muscles from your exercise unwinding a little. Jill, why don't you take her up there and make sure that she sits in that hot tub until she's relaxed. And, Jill. We all know what a tease you are. You let the boys put their hands anywhere as long as you are sure it's only their hand they are putting on you. I'll bet you're still a virgin."

"No, I am not a virgin. I just have to keep my body for the right man. I have more urges than the rest of you. I just don't want to take something home that I didn't bargain for. Mary Lee, you are going to get pregnant or catch something before the semester is out."

"Mary Lee. Jill. Stop it. Mary Lee, just keep quiet or go to your room." Craig didn't know who the speaker was and didn't find out. She was not that attractive, though not unattractive. The girls seemed to follow her orders though. She must be their sorority president or whatever they call it. She was a little older than most of the others.

He was enjoying this game. It was risky, though not seriously so. He could basically get by with just about anything with no danger to himself. They couldn't see him. If everyone in this sorority house knew of him, no one else would believe them. The authorities would threaten them with shutting down the house for illegal drug use. The ship would protect him from physical harm. Yes, he did believe in the ship now. He would never force himself on a girl, but the sexual playing with them might be fun. Sexual harassment? Lewd behavior? Peeping Tom? Impervious to prosecution.

Ship broke into his thought telepathically, *"Craig, you are in charge, but don't you think you are taking advantage of the power I have given you?"*

Craig thought back, "So. I'm a twenty year old healthy male. This is what I would call paradise. Butt out."

"This is exactly why some of the Captains lost their power quickly. The only reason I haven't cut you off is because there is not time to find another Captain. I will have to trust you not to take too much advantage of your power. There is a limit though."

Craig decided to sit back and listen and enjoy the view. He followed Dawn to her room to her bedroom where she proceeded to tell her roommate, Jill, about her experience walking home from the gym.

Dawn said, "Maybe I am going crazy, but I have a feeling that this invisible man may very well be watching. I know he was in the living room. On my way home I felt his hands holding mine and then he punched out some drunken frat rat that got a little crude toward me."

"Dawn, you're just hungry for a man. You haven't had a boyfriend or a real date since you've been here. It's perfectly natural to start imaging things when you get that hungry."

"Jill. Shame on you. I just haven't met the right guy. Actually, I'm not even looking. I want to get my degree to fall back on before I get tied up with a man. I am not hungry."

"Dawn. If I had an invisible man, I would have him living with me every night. I could go with others and let them turn me on and then go to bed with him every night without anyone knowing that I'm getting it regularly and calling me a slut. An invisible man can't give you anything, but pleasure. You're not a virgin are you?"

"No, Jill. But that's when I decided I would get my education. I had a boyfriend that dumped me after he told me that I was the only one. Then he went home for the summer and sent me a wedding invitation for him and a high school sweetheart."

"That's stupid, Dawn. I'll tell you what. If I find something that feels like a man in here that I can't see I'll make love to him right here. Okay. Actually, maybe I should get me a vibrator to go to bed with. Your imagination is going wild. There is no such thing as the invisible man. That was just a work of fiction. Besides, the invisible man went nuts and became dangerous."

"No. He protected me from that drunk. His touching me felt gentle ... no tender ... careful ... almost loving. He likes looking at us, but I don't think he is dangerous. It's just that there is no privacy from him. You can't tell when he is there."

Dawn said, "If you are here will you take my hand?"

Craig moved toward her, careful to not get too close and reached out to hold her hand in his.

"Jill, meet my invisible man. Hold your hand out like I did." She pulled her hand back. Jill cautiously held out her hand.

Jill started to jerk her hand free, but when he held tighter than she expected she relaxed and left her hand in his. "Do you get your jollies by ogling young girls? Are you some horrible space creature with a human feeling body and sounding voice?"

"No."

"Some dirty old man from another planet?"

"I'm a nineteen year old college student here at the university with some unusual capabilities. I just learned how to do this and think it's neat to be able to go and do without being seen."

Dawn said, "I thought you said twenty?"

"I will be twenty in April."

Jill, now much more courageous than she had been asked, "May I move in and feel your face and body to see if you are human?"

".... Uh... Yeah, why not."

Jill was very attractive. He still liked Dawn better, but he really was a nineteen year old college student and at that age a lot of girls are attractive. She moved her hands up his arm to his shoulder and then lightly up his neck to his face. She then moved her body in next to his and put his hand on her buttocks and then her arms around his neck and pulled him down for a kiss that turned into a French kiss. Then as they were kissing and she was moving her body against his, she lowered one hand to his buttocks and then to his fly where she grasped him.

He pulled away from her, moving her hands away and stepping away.

She then asked, "Why?"

He mumbled, "Why what? Uh. Because I'm shy. Even when I'm invisible, I still feel self conscious."

Dawn said, "Jill. Do you realize how ridiculous you look making out with thin air?"

"If you close your eyes, you could swear he was there." She said softly into his ear, "Better come back and see me when I am alone in the privacy of my room. I could hardly imagine what it would be like to have an invisible man living in my room. Can invisible men get anyone pregnant?"

"Yes."

"Shit. You're lying. If you're not really here how can you leave anything behind?"

Craig said, "I guess I can't explain it. If I were to spit on the patio, the spit would be visible. Does that explain?"

Dawn asked, "Can you appear so that we can see you?"

"Yes, I could, but then you would be able to identify me."

"Dawn asked, "What about finger prints or other evidence?"

"They leave with me?"

Jill said, "Then when you left you wouldn't leave us pregnant. Right?"

"You're right... but I would have to remember to make all traces disappear."

Jill asked, "You aren't carrying anything catching are you?"

"No, I'm not. I am impervious to all Earthly diseases."

Dawn asked, "Does that mean that you have the capability of ending disease on Earth? Are you from Earth?"

"First question. Yes I could eliminate disease, but I can't do it for everyone without improving the science on Earth to have the capability of manufacturing the necessary medicine. I could not manufacture enough serum for the Earth and there is no way that I could dispense it alone. Second question. My family came from England to the United States prior to the revolutionary war. I was born in Oklahoma. I only got my capabilities a few days ago."

Dawn asked, "Do the other members of your family have this capability?"

"No, I am the only one in the world right now although there has always been one person with this capability?"

"Why haven't the others changed the world?"

"Many have changed the world. They tried in their ways, but the world wasn't ready. Some wasted their power for money. Most could not handle the power. Aristotle, D'Vinci, Ben Franklin, Edison, Pasteur to name a few. Nicola Tesla was a prime Captain of the ship, but everyone treated him like he was crazy. If Edison had his way we would be using DC power instead of AC power. Actually Tesla had the Ship science almost developed to broadcast power into the air to make electricity free to everyone and have airplanes that would fly on broadcast electricity just like the Atlanteans. He hurried his experiments too much and blew a hole in Siberia in one of his last tests. You've heard about the huge blast in Siberia that leveled trees for miles. Well, he broadcast too much power from one location. It heated the ionosphere to the point that it basically became a mirror for the broadcast power which focused the power on Siberia and, well, many scientists think it was a collision with anti-matter. It wasn't. He invented radio you know, even though Marconi got the credit for it. He was too early. However, his family later got the patent changed to show it was invented by Tesla. He had the backing of J. P. Morgan for years of experiments. Anyway, he tried to go too fast and ended up with everyone thinking he was nuts. When he went too far, he lost his abilities and died with untold information that could have made a huge difference to the world. Fortunately, science has come a long way since Tesla's time. I have a mission to advance science 100 years per year of actual time for the next 10 years, or I will be the last."

"Why the last? What's going to happen?" asked Dawn.

"I'm sorry. I shouldn't have told you what I have. You should live a normal life unless you are in a position to make a major difference to the world." Craig was definitely cooling off at the barrage of Dawn's questions.

"What makes you think you are in the same class with Aristotle and Tesla?"

"Actually, I'm not, but I'm what the world has now, for better or for worse."

Dawn asked, "Then why are you here chasing after me and playing with Jill when you should be changing the world?"

Wow, was he turned off now. Strange to be standing there with a very gorgeous girl he thought he was in love with a few moments ago, and not be aroused. "Long story. To have an effect on the world I have to have credibility. I figure that a University awarding a doctorate degree in minimum time would give me some notoriety that would give me credibility to have people listen. I am waiting for the results of my application for the award of a doctorate degree from OU."

"And how long have you been here at the University of Oklahoma?" Jill asked.

"Three semesters."

Dawn asked, "What were your grades?"

"Two point eight, but I did score a 98 percentile on the ACT. My advisor talked me into taking 26 semester hours plus the regular non-credit classes my first semester. Then I had to take a part time job for money, and my grades slipped."

Dawn asked, "As a freshman?"

"Yes."

"So what makes you think that you are going to skip the bachelor's degree and get a doctorate." Dawn asked.

"Because I challenged the professors to ask a question I couldn't answer and then gave some of them some scientific breakthroughs to check out improvements to what they thought were their own secret research.'

Jill asked, "And just how did you get this chance."

"I took the most CLEP tests anyone had ever taken for several days in a row. I got a perfect score on all of them."

Dawn asked, "And just how did you get so smart? I had a three point eight five grade point average last semester."

"I told you. I've only had this power for the last few days."

Dawn asked, "And just where did you get this power?"

"You wouldn't believe me if I told you, and I am not allowed to tell. Maybe someday. Maybe then, you will be able to see for yourself and become my helper. Right now, pure chance has put us together. I don't know you well enough and you don't know me."

"That's right. I'm not so sure that I want to know you either. Why don't you just go upstairs with Jill and leave me alone to think."

Craig said, "I think that I'd better go before we are all sorry."

Dawn said, "Whatever."

Jill said, "I don't usually invite boys to my room. In fact, I'm a virgin. I just like to turn men on and have them turn me on. I would like being turned on all the time. I do not let them do anything. I don't want to catch anything or get pregnant before I get married. However, I am safe on both counts with you. Come on. Let's have some fun. I promise you won't get pregnant either."

Craig thought, "Ship, take me out of here."

"I will never question another crazy story you have Dawn. Do you believe his story?"

Dawn said, "I don't know what to think or believe. I am a little overwhelmed. I feel like I must be on some kind of drugs. Do you have this kind of thing happen when you smoke marijuana or snort cocaine?"

Jill said, "How would I know. I've never taken illicit drugs and I really don't drink that much. I only pretend to get drunk so some boy will come on to me. That way when the petting gets too heavy I can pretend to come to my senses and firmly say no without hurting their feelings, or just pretend to pass out."

Dawn said, "I'll be in my room thinking the rest of the night."

Jill said, "I'll be in my room humping my pillow. I really did want him to come to my room. Feeling an invisible guy and imagining having really safe sex with someone you can't see was really a turn on."

Craig said to himself or to Ship, "I think I should continue my shopping expedition. It's not like being a peeking Tom, is it? The opportunity to roam the girl's dorms and sororities inspecting the girls naked is just too much temptation. Besides, I know that girls liked to look at guys too. In fact, in junior high, I caught some girls looking through a hole in the wall in the boys shower room in the basketball gym. Since you, Ship, told me I should have a wife, I need to be looking for a life mate for this adventure. I also believe that I need help in this mission. I can not bring a man on board, but you allow a wife, not a girl friend. Not just a female scientist, but a wife. With all of the work I have to do to advance science so quickly, I don't have much time to find this help mate. I really need human advice, not just Ship's. I don't even trust my own thoughts."

"I need to make an inventory of what I want in a girl. I want one the most beautiful girls in the world. I want someone intelligent to help me. I don't just want sex or I would not still be a virgin, but I do want sex so she had to not just be the brainy type that might not be able to handle it. I need someone practical but smart. I really liked Dawn, but love at first sight is not necessarily the answer. She had a fantastic body, she was smart, she seemed to think like I would want a wife to, but then she turned me off with her questions. Besides, I don't think it is mutual. She didn't seem at all attracted to me. I haven't really looked around much.

There had been some girls in high school that wanted to take my virginity, and there had been some girls that I would have done anything to do it with, but the two circumstances had conspired to leave me a virgin. I've never tried looking at girls as something other than just dates. Looking for a wife, now, is a lot different."

"I think my next visit will be to the Delta Gamma sorority at the other end of the sorority fraternity row and right across from the main campus versus on sorority row. Ship."

Ship said, *"Why don't you let me use my databanks to find you the right women?"*

"No thanks, I can look for myself. Take me there in look only mode." He was there in the main living room, invisible, but there. There were basically four modes, observe, look, invisible or virtual mode, and visible. Observe was just watch on a television screen and listen over speakers. Look was actually partial teleportation, but not solid enough to really be there. He could see and hear, but not touch, smell, or taste. Invisible was the same as being there in fully body, except invisible. Then of course was full teleportation where the atoms of his body were wholly moved to the new location and reassembled just like on Star Trek.

"It's eleven o'clock now and some of the girls are going to bed. Some of the girls are probably in their rooms studying. Some are just reading. Some are together talking in their rooms. Some are watching television. And some are coming in from Thursday night dates. Okay, what now?"

The minute they saw a man, he would be thrown out. He went first without body, in look mode, just to see what was going on without any danger of being bumped into. There were already two girls that knew about him. They maybe knew too much. He'd have to keep his mouth shut more. As soon as he got his early degree and started making a name, they would know who he was and could make things unpleasant. However, to find a wife, he would have to talk with them to find out about them. Right now he was just window shopping.

"I can't tell much from a bunch of girls watching television in a group or sitting around together reading or studying. I need to make a tour of the upstairs bedroom first. I'll just go up the stairs and down the hall to look in the open doors." He went into some of the rooms to inspect a good looking girl and listen in to see what type of girl they were by the conversation. He then went back down the hall once to check for additional girls that might have come up when he was in a room. He then asked the computer to keep a check and entered some rooms to see the girls closed in their rooms. He went invisible instead of virtual mode.

He found some too fat or too skinny. Red heads typically had too fair a skin and Craig was a sun lover. Some were freckled. Some wore thick glasses that took away from their looks. Some were druggies and had an "out of here" look. Some drank too much.

"Now, this one looks promising." Craig thought to himself. "Let's just move in a little closer to the bed. She looks pretty good lying on her stomach on the bed reading a book. Her legs are slender and soft, not bony or fat. Her waist is tiny. Her blond hair is long, probably to her shoulder blades if she were standing. Now, her hair came nearly to her waist in back and draped down on her pillow like blinders to block out her vision to the sides while she read the book in front on her on the pillow as she rested her chin on her hands. The book was "Chains of Command" written by Dale Brown. I've read that book. I'm a little surprised by a girl reading a male war book. I can smell her hair. It's clean and fresh, not soapy. I can't see her face wrapped in all that blond hair."

She felt his presence and stopped reading. He backed away as she rolled over to look his way. She had to flip her long hair to one side to look his direction. She had a beautiful face. She saw nothing so went back to reading her book. Craig backed off and looked around her room. She had other military stories and science fiction books. He was interested. She wasn't muscled like Dawn, but she was very attractive and maybe they shared some common interests.

"Ship. Put me here, in virtual mode." Craig sat in a chair across the room. He said, "Excuse me."

The girl turned around to look at the door. "Okay, who has a boy in here? It's after hours."

"I like her voice. It's soprano, but not squeaky, and sounds soft and kind of sexy." Craig replied out loud, "You are the one that has the boy in here."

"What? Where are you? Who, are you?"

Craig kept his silence as she got out of bed and stood up, looking around the room and over the end of the bed. He thought, "She is very busty. She looks pretty good wearing that silk or nylon pajamas with loose fitting shorts and a short sleeve shirt. The shirt is loose and hides her except around her bust where the buttons are pulled. She must be at least a D cup." Craig thought.

She leaned over the end of the bed to check it out. As she leaned over he could see that her breasts were really big. She got down and checked under the bed. She then walked to the closet and checked inside moving her clothes from side to side. She then checked her private bathroom, finding nothing. Craig closed the door on her and then stood back against the wall out of the way. She opened it and looked around the room. She went to the windows to check that they were closed and locked.

"All right where are you hiding?" She wasn't afraid.

Craig said, "Promise you won't get scared?"

She jumped and then said, "No. I'm not a scaredy cat. I just want to know where you are and what you think you are doing here."

"I am not visible to you. You know the story of the invisible man?"

She was startled again, but not scared. "Yes. But I don't believe it."

Craig said, "Don't get scared. I'm not here to hurt you. I would like to talk. Stand in front of the mirror so you can see behind you. Close your eyes. I will come up behind you and put my hand on your shoulder. You keep your eyes closed and put your hand on mine. I will then put my other hand on your other shoulder. Put your other hand on that one. I will then gently massage your shoulders and you can open your eyes. That way you will know by touch that I am here, but invisible. Okay?"

She hesitated and then moved in front of the mirror and said, "I'm ready."

Craig moved up behind her and as soon as she closed her eyes he placed his hand on one shoulder as promised. She gave a start, but kept her eyes closed and placed one hand on his. They did the same with the other shoulder and opposite hands.

Craig said, "Okay open your eyes."

She did, but of course could not see him. She spread her legs so she could see behind them in the full length mirror on the bathroom door.

She said, "Can I turn around?"

"Yes." He started to pull his hands free.

She said, "No, don't move." She pirouetted around and moved toward him, still holding his hands. His hands ended up over her shoulders. She moved in and put her arms around his waist. Her shoulders were the perfect height to fit under his shoulders. Her nylon or silk pajamas left little to the imagination as her overly large breasts pressed on his lower ribs.

"Yes, you are there aren't you? Stay right where you are." She locked her door and turned up her stereo. "So no one will hear your voice" She then stood in front of him about a foot from where he had been standing. She was short enough and close enough, that Craig could see her considerable cleavage down the front of her pajama tops. Her breasts stood out on their own, without much sag for their size. "Now, don't take this personal. Are you human?"

Craig answered, "Yes."

"Are you from Earth? Can you appear in person, I mean such as I could see as well as feel you? Are you a scientist that has discovered invisibility like in the "Invisible Man"? Can you completely control it? How old are you?"

"Nineteen, and yes to the other questions."

"Do you go to college?"

"Yes, right here at the University of Oklahoma."

"Will you appear so I can see you?"

"Not yet. I would like to get to know you before I let you see me?"

"I believe you. I think. I need to do some more checking." He had a healthy teenage desire for sex. The girls he wanted to do it with were either not available, in the wrong place at the wrong time, like the costume room backstage with people that might walk in on them, or they were girls that came on to him that he did not want to do it with. He was instantly aroused and she was aroused by all this. She then put his arms around her waist and guided him backwards. He staggered back until he tripped on the foot of her bed. She sat on him near the foot of the bed.

"No. I'm not ready for that." he gasped back.

She said, "Just as well. I've never made love to an invisible man. It really turned me on."

He couldn't believe that he had retreated from such a gorgeous girl. He said, "I'm sorry. I don't even know your name."

"Sarah."

"Sarah what?"

"You first."

"I'm sorry, I have to go. I'm not ready to reveal who I am yet." She was kissing him when he zapped back to the ship. He looked back into her room. Sarah had gone back to her bed, rolled over onto her back and was lying there spread eagle with her mountainous breasts rolling to each side as she breathed deeply. He did not listen in. She definitely was not fat. Her hips were narrow, her legs shapely, her waist was very narrow and laying on her back her rib cage was clearly visible. She had taken his leaving in stride. He rested for hours. He woke in the ship. When he checked the time he discovered it was Friday at ten o'clock in the morning.

Ship asked, *"Why did you want to get away from her? No other men retreated in all of history."*

"I can't believe that. What about during Puritan times?"

4 WORKING FOR A PHD

He had missed one class. He decided to miss the rest of the day of his regular classes and have some fun with the professors. He went to Professor Gimble's graduate class in microbiology and walked in a few seconds before the class started. The other students saw him enter. He took a seat toward the back of the room. When ever the professor asked a question, Craig answered. After the third answer, the professor identified him and asked him to leave.

That was not a smart move. Rather than disrupt a class again, he went into the mathematics classroom prior to the most advanced doctorate math theory seminar and wrote a complex equation on the board. Ship gave him this equation based on what the day's seminar discussion was supposed to cover. He signed his name at the bottom. He then watched the class discussion using virtual reality. The professor and students all copied the equation. They had been working on the development of this formula for six weeks and then a non-math student, not in the doctorate program had written a formula that provided new answers in a different method. He rescheduled class for the week giving them instructions for the next week to find any holes in the formula. The professor wrote down Craig's name after the formula. If the formula was correct, and it appeared to be, it was going to change a number of concepts which could to lead to a major improvement in astronomical predictions as well as sub-atomic particle research. He would have to find out more about this Craig fellow. He knew every student in graduate level mathematics and none were on this level.

Craig went from there to the aeronautical lab. They were preparing a new model for testing in the wind tunnel. It was mounted in the tunnel already. It was the fourth day of testing. Craig removed that model, installed one created by the ship and with Ship's instruction ran the wind tunnel to its maximum speed that it could operate continuously. He had to be visible in order to see his own hands for more delicate work, like attaching the model. He then went back to the ship to watch the reaction. It was only moments before the dean, several other professors, and several students entered the wind tunnel lab to see who was messing with their experiment.

Professor Davis, the dean of Aeronautical Engineering said, "Who has been messing with our model. This promised to be the most important breakthrough in the university's history. This was going to put our school on the map. Someone shut down the tunnel."

"No keep the power on. Professor. Come look at this. The tunnel is generating the maximum six hundred miles per hour, but the drag on this model is less than .1 gram. Do you realize how little power it would take in the go fast department?"

"Yes, I do Ken. Let's check the rest of the readings and then check the gauges. They changed the angle of attack of the model to measure lift. This is phenomenal." After they had recorded the readings, they changed the tunnel speed to test from maximum to minimal speeds. They were astounded. When they got to zero speed, they read the model weight. Professor Davis said, "Okay. Relax. We've wasted our time. Someone has destroyed all of our gauges. According to the gauge this model only weighs 3 grams. It would have to be of aluminum foil to weight that amount and aluminum foil could not withstand any speed at all. Ken. Just get that model out of there and get our model back in. We need to check out the whole system to see how much damage was done. I'll be back in an hour. The rest of you stay here and see if there is some easy fix."

"Professor. Come back. Feel this model."

"This *is* light weight. I'm surprised you didn't crush it getting it out. Wait. I ... can't even bend a wing. What is this thing made out of? There is some writing on the bottom. It says, "made by Craig Decker"." Isn't he the one that challenged the system?"

Ken, the doctoral student, said, "Who? He's not in Aeronautical Engineering. I've never heard of him."

Professor Davis said, "Never mind. Here, I'll help with our model. Don't touch anything. Let's check the readings with our model." There testing went on for an hour. "Gentlemen. This Craig Decker just put this university on the map. Our model is like the Wright brother's Kitty Hawk flyer compared to a B-2 stealth bomber in comparison. It's made out of some unknown alloy that weighs about as much as Styrofoam, but has strength. Our model had 20 kilograms of drag before it came apart at a lower speed than Craig Decker's model. Put this Craig Decker's model back in and continue the testing. Put it through anything you know. Different angles of attack versus lift and drag, you know what to do. I'm going over to the metals lab and grab Professor Myrtle and get him back here for some metallurgy ideas."

In thirty minutes the two deans were back. Professor Myrtle knew the metal as soon as he picked up Craig's model wind tunnel airplane. "Professor Davis, this Craig Decker gave me some new things to add to a new alloy I was working on. I was upset at first that the metal exploded in size to ten times its original mass as it cooled. When cool it was extremely light weight and I thought about just throwing it away as another bad idea. Then I found that it seemed extremely strong. I have not slept since

Thursday afternoon and the meeting with the university president and this Craig Decker. I have taken that metal sample and tried to bend, twist, press, and melt it. I even tried the laser beam. It seems to be impervious. I knew from the small sample I had originally made its approximate expansion so I made some more and put it in a mold ten times the size of the molten metal. It cooled to fill the mold without hurting the mold. I didn't completely test it, but it seemed as good as the original. I then tried putting it in a smaller mold. Again, it cooled to exactly fill the mold. Even though it only had expansion of five times, the sample weighed the same as the original sample for the amount of alloy injected into the mold. I made a one kilogram sample. Put it in a mold that allowed no expansion. It did not break the mold, but it weighed the same amount of another one kilogram amount in a mold that allowed a ten times expansion. Both samples appear indestructible. I can't even scratch them with a diamond. The drawback is that you cannot weld it or in any way hurt it with heat. In fact it appears to be a perfect insulator. It won't get hot or cold either. What have you done with this model?"

Professor Davis said, "We have put this model through every bit of testing that we could think of. Its aerodynamic properties are like no other thing in existence. A full size jet liner or cargo plane that would normally weigh four hundred thousand pounds would, by my calculations, would only weigh four thousand pounds empty and would be able to fly six hundred miles per hour with a small jet engine like that on a cruise missile. The fuel savings alone would be unbelievable. If it is also indestructible, we could build an airplane that could fly forever without replacement. It could not be hurt by hail or bird strikes, or even, from, say, mid air collisions. It wouldn't be too good for the passengers to have a mid air collision, but the airplane would survive. Can you imagine a jet engine made of this material? How about a space shuttle? Of course, nothing is indestructible. But still... What about fatigue?"

Professor Myrtle said, "I have no way to test for fatigue of this metal. I was not able to bend or twist with anything in our lab. Maybe in another lab, but not ours."

Professor Davis said, "Who is this Craig Decker?"

"He started taking massive amount of CLEP tests and scored perfect on all of them. When he wanted more he was brought in to the president and the president called in several of us deans. This Craig Decker then demanded an award of a doctorate degree and challenged the deans to come up with a question that he could not answer. He answered all of the questions. He then gave me some elements to add to a new alloy I was working on and challenged me to try it. He suggested some new additives to a new antibiotic. The president ordered us to try them out and meet in his office one week from that day with this Craig Decker to decide if he should get this honorary degree. Craig Decker said that he had to make some important breakthroughs and he needed a doctorate and a university to back him up in getting the things into production. He threatened to go elsewhere if he didn't get his way."

"I plan to be there too. It sounds like we had better award his degree today, if it were up to me."

Professor Myrtle said, "You don't understand. This kid is a nineteen year old sophomore that only had a C average last semester. He says he only recently acquired this knowledge and what he has given us is only for starters. I did check him out some. He scored in the Mensa range on the ACT and he was working his way through school up until a few weeks ago. Then he won the Texas State Lottery a few days ago."

Professor Davis said, "I don't care. After seeing this model, I would award him a doctorate in Aeronautical Engineering today, if he were here. You can count on my company next Friday in the president's office. I want him to explain the hows and whys of this incredible model. Wait, you say he won the lottery and got all this intelligence in the last week or so? Did he give any explanation?"

"I'll endorse him myself. This new metal could dramatically decrease the cost of anything made of metal. Automobiles, engines that don't wear out ... your aircraft, ships that can carry far more. The only drawback is that molding it is the only method we have of forming it. It would have to be molded with bolt holes in it to attach doors and things. The molds would have to be very accurate. We would also have to mold the bolts in order to maintain strength. Can you mold in perfect threads to a bolt and a nut? I don't know. I just want to know where it came from."

Professor Davis said, "Let's call Professor Gimble and ask him about his gift from this Craig Decker."

"Hello, Doctor Gimble."

"Sound sleepy. This is Doctor Myrtle if we are using titles today. How is your antibiotic coming?"

"Well. It's too early to tell anything. Actually it takes years to bring a new antibiotic to the public. Something about the additive that Craig Decker gave me seems to kill the HIV dead in its tracks in a Petri dish, and it looks promising so far. I'm running a control using my old antibiotic to make sure that it's the additives. How is your new alloy?"

Professor Myrtle excitedly told him about his results to date and then handed the telephone to Professor Davis who told him about the model with Craig Decker's name on it. Their conversation sparked new interest in Professor Gimble's attitude that was apparent through the telephone. "Yes, I have to admit that preliminary tests indicate that a major change was made in my research. It will take months to know for sure, but I am going to inject some HIV infected rats immediately. I'll let you know the results before our meeting next week. If you will pardon me, I have a lot of work to do.

5 SPYING

Now that Craig had tried out both virtual reality and invisibility mode he decided to see if he could use it to spy on foreign enemies of the United States. He decided to test it out in a safer mode by blinking into France to start with. That way he could test the language translation of the ship in addition to the invisibility he had already tested. He didn't know where to appear. The French government took weekends off also. What came to mind was the Moulin Rouge.

He zapped to the street outside just to see what it looked like. It was a nightclub that looked like a Dutch windmill. It was painted in red. There were limousines pulling up and letting people out. Most of the clientele looked fairly wealthy. It must be near show time because people seemed to be converging on it. Suddenly he was back in the ship. "What happened?"

"Instant replay." The big screen in the command room showed Craig standing in the middle of the street looking at the cabaret when a stream of cars approached. Craig could see himself standing there on the replay although people could not see him. Because the traffic could not see him he saw ten cars one after the other pass through the spot where Craig had been. The ship had protected him from harm that Craig had not even seen. He had asked for the street out front so that's what he got. He

preferred going in body rather than just looking in. He stayed past the changing of a traffic light and Ship brought him back to the ship. Because it was more than one car the ship had not been able to blink him back immediately. It was nice to know the ship was watching out for him.

He winked back to the dressing room of the Moulin Rouge. The dressing room was surprisingly crowded with near naked girls bumping into him repeatedly. They bumped into each other so much they didn't even notice bumping into something warm but invisible. Craig could hear all of their words in English, but not enough to understand with all of the noise.

"Ship, I want to be transported to someplace in the U.S. government where they are discussing some kind of international crisis. I want to see what's going on." Craig found himself in a room filled with generals and the president of the United States.

The President said, "So you are telling me that there is nothing we can do about the situation?"

An Army general said, "No sir. We no longer have enough military to fight another Gulf War but with Iran. They have replaced their old tanks that with the latest Russian models that were sold cheaply on the open market with the breakup of the Soviet Union, as cheap as five thousand dollars from some of the old Soviet Block countries. We know that a number of nuclear warheads were missing from the Soviet inventory. Besides, even if we did have the men and equipment we had back in 1990; it took us months then to build up a force in Saudi Arabia."

The President replied, "What are the probabilities that the Iranian leader will start another war?"

A civilian spoke from the other end of the long table, "Sir, we feel that it is very high that something will start within the week. The Iranians are on full alert with everyone having already reported in for duty as near as we can tell. Their aircraft are standing alert. By the way Sir, let me remind you that almost the entire Irarqi Air Force never lost its fully capable status during the Gulf War. They simply taxied their aircraft into the towns and cities parking them next to hospitals and schools to prevent us catching them on the ground. Many were flown to Iran. Iraq and Iran seem to be friends. They have long since rebuilt all of their runways and shelters."

Craig went back to the ship to sleep and then decided to go to visit the Iranian leader. He zapped into the middle of a military meeting off to the side of the room. The room was constructed entirely of gray concrete. The only color was the khaki uniforms and the medals of the people around a huge oak table. The chairs were red velvet. One of the military members at the side of the table was saying to the Iranian leader, "Your Holiness. If we use a nuclear bomb on Tel Aviv, the Allied Forces may use nuclear weapons and bomb us into oblivion."

The Iranian leader retorted, "General Jamil, they would not dare do that. We have shelters for all of our key people. They would only be killing civilians. They would not do that."

"But, Sir. We will be killing millions of Jews."

"That is the point. Is it not? We will make it known that we have purchased thirty or more nuclear warheads from the Russian territories. We have modified our Scud missiles to deliver them. From the so called Gulf war we showed them they could not find all of our missiles. After all the so called U.N. inspections we will show them they found nothing. Our under ground factories are still producing missiles and now that we have nuclear warheads. Our Scuds may not be able to threaten Europe, but we can hit Tel Aviv, anywhere in Syria, the northern half of Saudi Arabia, and most of Iran."

Another member from the other side of the table spoke up, "How are we going to be able to hide the launchings from the U.N. inspectors?"

"What inspectors? You General will be responsible for

eliminating them."

Craig spoke out, "You are a mad man. What makes you think that you can do this? Do you want your country turned to glass?"

Everyone in the room looked toward the voice. The Iranian leader said, "I thought this room was secure and now I find that it is not only bugged, but has some fool using speakers to talk to us. Who is responsible for this?"

Craig appeared so he could be seen as a hologram. He was dressed in his Jeans and Union Bay sweatshirt, obviously American except for his perfect Arabic, "I did."

"Seize him" Several generals jumped at the Iranian leader's command and ran to within ten feet of Craig's image and then hit an invisible wall bouncing back into each other like Keystone Cops. Craig did not like the idea of someone passing through him in the hologram state and had asked Ship for the force field.

Craig said, "Sorry,. You are out classed. I have a force field around me. If you attempt to harm any U.N. officials, you will find them also protected. I could detonate all of your nuclear weapons in their storage, if you insist on trying to use them."

"This is some kind of American trick that their spies installed in this conference room." To Craig the Iranian leader said, "You can do nothing."

Craig said, "I would rather not detonate nukes. What kind of demonstration would you like? How about a Scud melting on the production line?"

"You cannot do that."

"Stand by your telephone." Craig winked out to the ship and then to where Ship had detected the Scud production line. He picked a Scud away from people and used a beam weapon that Ship had provided to him to fire at the Scud that immediately caught fire with the metal itself burning. Craig had overestimated the power needed and spread out the beam to melt more of the missile without it catching fire. Some Iranians ran toward it and some away from it.

Craig spoke through an amplification device over the noise. "Call the Iranian leader at 01 318 455 5562 and tell him what has happened. Do you understand me?"

An officer that looked like he was in charge agreed quickly as he looked toward the vacant spot where the voice was coming from and where the visible beam had come from.

Craig winked back to the Iranian leader's conference room. He said, "It's done." No one spoke again until the telephone rang.

"What? Slow down. A beam of light appeared from nowhere and first focused on a Scud. The metal caught fire at a small point ten centimeters wide and then the beam spread to cover most of the missile which promptly crumpled on itself. A voice gave you this number. Pah. You have fallen for an American trick."

Craig said, "Call one of your tank commanders and have him pick a tank for me to destroy. Please tell him to have the crew get out. I will destroy it while he is on the telephone to show you the power of this small beam weapon." Craig showed him the small funny looking handgun that looked like a toy with a small LED light.

The Iranian leader called, waited, and then spoke to a commander in the field. Craig winked back to the ship which found the tank that the commander had picked. The tank was manned.

Craig winked back to the conference room and told the Iranian leader, "I told you to evacuate the tank. Do it now." Craig fired his beam weapon for a second at the steel blast door of the conference room. A baseball size hole quickly appeared halfway through the foot thick door. It created an acrid smelling smoke.

The Iranian leader said on the telephone, "Evacuate the tank and watch it closely. I want you to report what you see as it happens."

Craig listened in as he reappeared near the tank. The tank commander was speaking, "A young man has appeared. Do you want me to shoot him?"

The Iranian leader replied, "Kill him with tank fire." As the tanks fired Craig winked back to the ship automatically and then reappeared in the conference room.

"Let me get on with my demonstration before I get mad. This shield protects me from people and I will automatically disappear from any danger."

The Iranian leader drew his forty five pistol and fired. Craig winked to the ship. The bullet from the Iranian leader's automatic caromed around the metal walls of the conference room sending everyone to the floor including the Iranian leader. He then winked to the vicinity of the tank but in invisible mode. He fired his beam weapon on full power. The voice on the Iranian leader's speaker phone said, "A beam appeared out of nowhere. The tank is glowing. No a two meter hole appeared all the way through the tank just as all of its fuel and explosives cooked off. What was it? I didn't see a person this time."

"Launch one." the Iranian leader said.

Craig had obviously come in late on this situation. The Iranian leader had apparently already launched a Scud. Craig flashed back to the ship. Craig said, "Ship, can you shoot it down?"

"Of course."

"Do so."

"That would give away my position. I would prefer that you shoot it down

using the remote ship. I will follow my order and shoot it down if you cannot. We still have over five minutes to intercept."

Craig had forgotten his training; there was a one man ship on the top deck. He made a run for it. The hatch was open. As he jumped on the small wing into the cockpit he was not afraid of damaging the wing because the ship was made from the new alloy he had provided to the University of Oklahoma. The hatch closed as soon as he was in the pilot's seat. At the instant the hatch was closed, the outer door of the ship opened and the small ship was boosted out into space. Craig hit the throttle control that was very similar to the typical jet fighter. He had a stick for his other hand. The fighter ship shot downward at incredible speed.

Through mind link he knew his speed had gone from a relative speed of zero or eighteen thousand miles per hour orbital speed to a speed relative to the Earth of twenty thousand miles per hour in two seconds. He felt no acceleration but only the normal gravity of the ship which was similar to Earth at sea level at twenty-nine point nine millibars of atmospheric pressure, but he could see the acceleration. It was like flying a video game with built in motion simulators. He could feel some acceleration, but the laws of physics would have made him a grease spot on the seat back without the artificial gravity. At the peak speed going toward Earth he was traveling at over one hundred thousand miles an hour. It was hard to tell on the speed meter because the acceleration and deceleration were a blur on the instrument. In twenty seconds he was into the atmosphere and had slowed to eight thousand miles per hour to match the speed of the Scud missile. He fired the destruction beam that took the total mass of the Scud missile and the Scud missile ceased to exist. It reappeared as mass for the ship to generate power back in space. The fuel, the body, the fins, the warhead, all appeared as compacted mass in the ship. By compacted, imagine taking an atom, stopping the electron, removing the space between the electrons and the nucleus of the atom and then packing all particles together with no space whatsoever. If the Scud were a separate piece of material instead of just being part of the mass, the entire missile would measure less than one hundredth of an inch square. The nuclear part of the warhead took as much space as the rest of the missile and its fuel due to the natural dense mass of plutonium.

Eight more Scuds were fired when the first one disappeared off the radar screen. Craig quickly turned toward Iran and the approaching missiles fired from eight different points. It took four minutes and twelve seconds for him to get into position and fire. He then flew slowly over a tank column at one thousand miles per hour. Because of the superb aerodynamics there was only a small sonic boom and very little dust kicked up. The tank crews saw it, but it didn't appear on any radars. The radios buzzed with their messages.

Craig stopped above the command bunker that still had the Iranian leader and his generals. Less than fifteen minutes had passed. He briefly fired his destructor and twenty feet of sand over the bunker disappeared leaving a sharp edged round hole twenty feet deep and ninety feet across. It took a three inch cube to store it in the ship. If the storage got full the excess would be spread as sand back on the earth in an isolated area. Craig was using a lot of energy so he was only storing only slightly more than he had used. He disappeared into the bunker conference room and said in perfect Arabic, "I think you better stop before I decide to vaporize this entire bunker."

The Iranian leader said, "I have already ordered my air force to destroy your ship. It is you that should run."

Craig was reassured that the small fighter was immune to anything that the Iranian leader had including nukes. Craig said, "Shall we watch?"

A big screen television appeared at one end of the conference room and they all watched as Iranian fighter planes fired missiles and guns at the ship. There was no apparent movement of the tiny ship. One MIG 31 dove directly into it. There was a huge ball of exploding jet fuel and explosive from the MIG 31. When the flame disappeared, the little fighter was still hovering perfectly motionless.

Craig said, "You are totally outclassed. The United States will have no more of your funny stuff. Now, I think I may just take you with me to stand trial for your crimes. You have twenty-four hours from now to surrender to the nearest U.N. team and confess your crimes or I will simply move you to a United States prison in the blink of an eye like I winked in and out of here. Remember, twenty-four hours and you cannot hide anywhere. Do not blame any of your people. The technology is beyond what you or your scientists can understand."

Craig was tired and winked back to the fighter and flew it back to the ship. It had not been hard work, but took a lot of adrenaline. The metal absorbed all radar and radio energy so it could not be followed. Back at the ship, Craig observed several meetings around the world on his handiwork. Everyone in the world new about the firings of the Scud missiles toward Tel Aviv and their subsequent disappearance in mid flight. The United States had satellite pictures of Craig's fighter firing the beam weapon at two of the Scuds and the firefight against the fighter as it hovered over the bunker.

General White in the National Military Command Center or NMCC in the Pentagon was speaking by telephone with the president. "Yes Mr. President, we have excellent pictures of some kind of small fighter aircraft that showed speeds in excess of twenty thousand miles per hour after shooting down the first Scud missile. It appears to measure eight feet long with a wingspan of only ten feet looking like our B-2 flying wing except with a strange shape. While we were taking pictures of the Scud this came down from a higher altitude at tremendous speed. It matched the speed of the Scud and then fired a beam weapon that made the Scud just disappear. I did say disappear, not blow up. It was just gone. As soon as other Scuds were fired it turned like an airplane but the distance to turn and the change from eight thousand miles an hour in one direction to over twenty thousand in the other would have been almost infinite G forces that would have broken any metal known, not to mention the pilot. No. We have no idea where it came from. It just appeared in satellite video that we were taking of the Scud missile. It came into view from above at a steep angle. We found it again destroying the fifth Scud that was destroyed. No Sir. The E-3 AWACS sentry aircraft that were tracking the Scuds and our radar satellites never saw it. There was no heat signature. When our AWACS reported fighters converging on a point inside of Iran, we focused our cameras and spotted the same fighter motionless over a perfectly round hole in the ground. The Iranian fighters fired everything they had at it and finishing with a MIG 31 finally ramming it Kamikaze style with no effect on it. It then hovered a few more minutes and then accelerated faster than our camera could track it going up. We lost it. No Mr. President. I do not believe in little green men coming out of space to protect Israel. Sir? What? Oh?"

Craig had appeared in the oval office facing the President. He had said, "Mr. President, I was the pilot of that aircraft."

After hanging up the telephone to the NMCC President Williams said, "How did you get in here?"

Craig said, "I just appeared here to explain a few things."

"What do you know about that aircraft?"

Craig said, "It is mine. It will fly into space for extended periods of time at speeds far in excess of the escape speed for earth orbit. It is made of a new metal that I recently gave to the University of Oklahoma. Check with Professor Myrtle. It gives the United States a new alloy almost impervious and well suited for space travel. I will not tell you the top speed because you would not believe me. I can not give you its technology yet because you are not ready for it. I would like to set up a meeting one month from today at twelve noon where I will tell you and your advisors what I need to do. Is that okay? Would you like to have the Iranian leader as a prisoner?"

When the President agreed, open mouthed, Craig disappeared back to the ship. The secret service burst into the oval office to find the President still standing there staring at nothing. One of them said, "Mr.

President. Are you okay?"

President Williams said, "Yes. Everything is fine. There is no problem."

"But Mr. President. You cut off your conversation with the NMCC and we heard another voice here."

"I said everything is fine. Call a full meeting of the cabinet in two hours."

Craig waited aboard the ship for the cabinet meeting and then looked in from the Ship. They went through the intelligence about the Scud missiles and the diminutive fighter plane that had shot them down or did they crash? Were they vaporized? How did that teenager appear in the oval office without anyone seeing him and how did he disappear in plain sight of the President. What was the purpose of the meeting the teenager called for? What did he mean perfect for space flight. Yes, he looked human. The small fighter was not of terrestrial design. There was some evidence that it went came from and went into space after the Scud encounter.

The President had already disturbed Professor Myrtle at the University of Oklahoma who hesitated to talk over the telephone. After FBI agents showed up at his door with a secure telephone called a STU-4v, he admitted, "A student gave me a formula for a new metal that appeared to be impervious to everything I could test it with. Yes, it is relatively easy to make and cures in a mold. It is lighter than any metal I have ever seen. Yes, I could give a sample to the military laboratories for testing if the university would retain its rights of discovery and get credit for publishing all papers on the metal. I want to be present to witness all testing of the new metal. We also have a new aerodynamic model from the same student that surpassed anything anyone has ever seen. "Yes sir, I will make sure that the model made out of apparently the same metal will be on its way to Tinker AFB, Oklahoma to be shipped to the wind tunnels at Arnold Air Force Station, Tennessee. Yes sir, it is small enough to fit in the back seat of an F15. Yes sir, I will also provide a sample made by the university will be taken to Tinker also to be shipped to the material labs at Wright-Patterson Air Force Base, Ohio. Yes sir, I would welcome taking both through every test available. They are far beyond anything we can test here."

The President knew the name of the teenager from the discussion, but was keeping it secret for now. Only the Vice President had been told the name. President Williams told the cabinet, "Gentlemen. It is my opinion that this person is far beyond our known science and may be extra-terrestrial, but appears human and apparently is on our side and not an enemy. I met with him in my office. If the tests of the model go as well as expected then we need to meet with this person sooner than the

one month meeting proposed by him.

6 SHOPPING FOR A MATE

Craig, on the other hand, had nothing more to do for now. He had averted the destruction of Israel by the Iranian leader. He had exposed his identity to the President of the United States that could identify him through the university. President Williams would test his model and his metal, but both would take time. That should convince the President. He had provided a mathematics breakthrough to help space travel through better calculations of star and atomic particle positions, aerodynamics for aircraft and eventually space craft, and a new form of metal. What else could he do? It was time to eat. He was an unknown so far. In general, he was unnoticed by the opposite sex. He didn't have the money for a fraternity before the Ship picking (rigging?) the Texas lottery and a lot of sorority girls were not interested in non-fraternity boys. None of the people that actually knew him knew that he had won the lottery. The non-sorority girls were there looking for money and everyone knew the fraternity boys had the money. Then there were the ones that were only interested in educations. He was only a sophomore. Most of the girls his age were looking for juniors or seniors in college... not another sophomore boy. Most of the dorms were coed anyway, but he figured he might as well put on his invisible mode and go looking. He decided to dispense with virtual reality. He could always zap away if he got into real trouble.

"Ship, monitor Dawn to make sure that she is protected and zap me to her if she has any trouble. I did promise to be her guardian angel, but I forgot. Take me to Walker Tower, girls' side, top floor, invisible mode."

He had decided to start at the top of the dorm and work his way down through eleven floors. The coed dorms shared a common central area, but there were four wings in each tower with one side of two wings being all girls and the other boys. Some of the girls had gone home for the weekend. Others had dates for which they were getting dressed and others were preparing to just go out and eat with their friends for the evening.

He started at one end of the X shape and walked to the other. He dodged girls coming down the hall singly, occasionally retreated, and sometimes entered a room to keep from being run into and discovered.

He saw one shapely girl coming down the hall in a tight tee shirt. He thought, "Now this could be fun." One room he retreated into had two fat girls in it. He made it down that side with the only interesting girl being the in the tight tee. He started down the other side when a group of girls came out of a room ahead and another group came in from the elevators. He dodged into the third room on the right. The girl in the room was naked except for her bikini panties. Craig closed the door behind him. She looked right at him and gasped, but of course saw nothing other than the door opening and closing. He dodged behind the door against the closet door as she went to the door and locked it. She was slender, but sexy. She did not have a big bust, but they were full for her size. She was about five foot four, six inches shorter than he was. Her hair was reddish brown, but she had a clear slightly tanned skin. There wasn't a single blemish that he could see. He could see the white outline of a small bikini. She reached for the closet door and almost touched him as he dove onto the bed. She heard it and probably saw the indentation on the bed and gasped again. Craig lay as still as he could so she wouldn't see the bed move more. She stood there looking at the bed as Craig stared back at her staring at him, or rather the bed. She was very slender, not skinny, just slender. Her hips were narrow, her waist maybe twenty inches. Her shoulders were narrow. She pulled out a large towel and wrapped it around her. She checked the door lock again and headed for the bathroom.

Craig realized that this wasn't right to sneak around like this. He didn't feel very horny and maybe should be more objective. The girl he was looking for had to like science. Not be overly concerned with helping the poor and oppressed. She needed to be physically fit as well as attractive. He didn't know what might happen and he was definitely headed for space, whether or not he could bring other ships from Earth with him. She still had to be sexy and somewhat small to attract him.

Craig said, "I have to get back to my experiment. It was fun." He disappeared from her bed, went out the door and moved down to the next floor.

He found only a couple of slightly overweight girls eating pizza in their room on that floor. As he found open rooms he looked at books that might give an indication of the interests of the girls therein. If he found one interested in science and maybe had a picture of her in the room, he might want to return.

After I check out the appearance, I must check the mind before making contact. He went down to the next floor. He found several girls home there and was able to walk into most rooms by going through the connecting bathrooms between each two rooms. The girls were in small enough groups he had now made it through two floors with no problem of detection. He also had found no girls he liked the appearances of. In checking for books and pictures in empty rooms he found nothing too exciting there either.

It was nearly 10 o'clock when he got caught. He had gone through one open room past the girls there to get to the next bedroom through the connecting bath. He had gotten a little cool and had pulled the unmade bed sheet over him as he lay on his back looking through a picture album trying to decide about the girl therein. He had decided to just rest his eyes after all the books he had gone through. He turned out the light for just a moment. He was on the fifth floor. He had found a few interesting girls based on the books, but few pictures of those girls in the rooms with interesting books. He laid the picture album down on the floor by the bed.

He woke up with some girl pulling back the sheet and climbing into the bed in the dark. He froze and looked. She was shapely in the moonlight. It appeared that she was entirely naked. In the picture album he had seen her grow from a little girl to glamour shots of herself. She was quite attractive. She had the right build that he was looking for that would be sexy, but looked very child bearing capable, if there is such a thing. She had blond hair that was over one shoulder and came to her breasts. There were pictures of her playing basketball in maybe early high school. There were pictures of her as a cheer leader at a cheer leaders' camp. He could see the moonlight on her blond hair. It must be her. After turning back the sheet she stretched with her arms and legs slightly spread eagled. She did have the body, if he could trust his vision in the moonlight streaming in through the window. She turned; sat on the edge of the bed and then stretched again on her back his time with her arms and legs straight this time. Her hands touched the wall and her legs were raised above the mattress by a few inches. She held that pose for what must have been three or four minutes. Yes. She was apparently physically fit. Craig knew almost any movement on his part would be detected by her. He took the chance and rolled off onto the floor with a thud.

She rolled off the bed on top of him pinning him to the floor. She grabbed his arms and forced them over his head. She was strong and Craig didn't fight her. It was very dark on the floor. He could see the silhouette of her blond hair, but otherwise almost nothing.

She said, "Who are you and what were you doing in my bed?"

"Your room was vacant and I was a little cool, so I covered myself up and went to sleep. I'm sorry."

"Well, get the hell out of my room. Now. How did you get in here and why are you here?"

"I walked in and I… "

"What were you doing in my room?"

"You wouldn't believe me if I told you."

"Try me or I'll scream and then watch the shit hit the fan. My door is unlocked and the whole dorm will be in here in seconds. I would have screamed already, but I can take care of myself and only scream under control."

"No. Please don't scream. I meant no harm. You really could never believe my story unless you turn on the light. Once you do you must promise not to scream and I will attempt some explanation."

She quickly moved away from him. "Are you deformed or grossly ugly?"

"No, but promise not to scream and turn on the light."

"Okay." She moved up to sit on his chest and holding his hands together, still over his head used her other hand to turn on the light on the headboard and of course saw nothing. The expression on her face was total astonishment. "Where did you go?" She immediately jumped off of him and back against the closet opposite the foot of the bed. "What's happening? Who, what are you?"

"I'm right here and I'm just another student turned invisible."

"Oh God. What in Hell? You're invisible!"

"Very observant. Now do you want to know why I was here?"

"Yes. Just stay where you are, wherever that is." She kept her position looking much lower than where his face was.

Craig got up and sat on the bed. "I'm sitting on your bed, as you can probably see. If you want to sit down, I'll tell my story. In the last few days I have gained some unreal power. I was told I need a wife to help me help the world with that power. I have a phenomenal mission to accomplish for the world and too little time. I need a wife quickly that can help me. Being an OU college student, I came here, looking. I figured I could look at pictures and school books to find out something about a girl without her knowing about me. I said I was in a hurry. I stopped in your room because I saw your textbooks included biology, zoology, and paleontology. I was looking through your picture album. First I got cold and pulled the sheet up. Then my eyes were hurting so I turned off the light to rest my eyes for just a moment, and apparently went to sleep."

"When was that?"

"Ten."

"Well. It is now eleven thirty. I came in the dorm an hour ago. I had gone to the bathroom when visiting a dorm mate down the hall so when I came in here I just stripped my clothes and went to bed without turning on any lights until now. Why am I talking to you? This is crazy. You can't be invisible. Your whole story is screwy. I wouldn't believe a word of it except that you are here and you are invisible. Maybe ***I*** am dreaming."

"No you are not dreaming. I am real. I am invisible because I am in a hurry to find a wife that can help me in a mission you would not believe. I have powers beyond being invisible." She was now on her knees with her upper body now propped up on her elbows on the side of the bed. The headboard light was perfect. He could see between her good size, C-cup?, breasts down her bony rib cage past her flat tummy to her fatless thighs. She had a body. Her long blond hair had been flipped to one side and the ends were over one shoulder and down her upper arm to just hit the bed on that side. Her eyes were a pale blue. She had an all over bronze tan so she must have either spent her Christmas break on a nude beach or under tanning lights.

"Where did you get these powers?"

"I can only tell my wife and then only if I choose the right wife."

"What is this mission you need help with?"

"Saving mankind."

"Are you one of those potted plant lovers who think that the world will end without conservation and free love?"

"God no. I believe that science has not been keeping up because we have spent too much time and money on welfare and pretty things when we should have been trying to spread mankind to the stars."

"Have you been in space? Or are you from space? Are you human?"

He avoided the first two questions, "Yes, I am human. Do you think that mankind has a need to go find other planets to live on?"

"Yes. I am a fan of Star Trek and I believe that man needs to colonize other planets, but it will not be in my lifetime."

"It has to be."

"What?"

"It is our generation that must get to the stars or mankind will be wiped out before they get there. That is my mission."

"And how are you going to do this?"

"Invisibility is only one power, but that is also why I need a wife to help me and talk about solutions with."

"I love talking about theory and potential scientific solutions. I don't believe that mankind will have a permanent colony anywhere for another hundred years or more. Are you saying you want me to marry you, ah, sight unseen?"

"No. Of course not. I am just looking for a potential wife now because I have a few days free before I have to get to work on my mission. That sounds pretty stupid, but it is true. I can't do much for another week except have some fun and look for a wife."

"What have you done so far?"

"I have given Professor... Sorry, I can't tell you what I've done or you might identify me. I'm not ready to be identified yet."

"Well. Let's see what we can do?" She climbed up on the bed on all fours. She found him by feel. She started at his head and worked down. She got up and backed up, standing in the bathroom doorway, she said, "Okay. That was for fun. Now get out of here. I liked your story. I have a tendency to believe you. I would like to help on such a mission if it had any chance of success whatsoever, but I'm not making love to any invisible person I can't see. I don't know if I've gone completely off my rocker or not. I happen to be a virgin and plan to stay that way until I get married. Now get out of here or I will scream the most coldly calculated scream you have ever heard then we will hunt you down and hold your invisible body for the campus police to figure out what to do with."

He opened and closed the door to the hall to show that he was leaving. He went to virtual reality mode and watched her. She did move like a cat. She walked around her bed waving her arms out wide spread and swinging her feet to make contact with him if he was there. She searched the room then locked both the hallway and the bathroom door. She went to the window and looked out the blinds. She went to the full length mirror on her closet door and looked at herself and the room behind her. She pinched herself and then said to herself, "That was one heck of a dream. My imagination really got away from me. I'd better start going to bed earlier. I went to sleep instantly. I remember doing my isometric exercise in bed. Then I felt the bed jerk and heard a thud. I rolled out of the bed in attack mode and there he was. I wonder what he would have looked like if he were really there. Now I'm talking to myself out loud. I give up. Tomorrow, I'll wake up and know this was a dream." She turned off the lights and went back to bed.

7 TAKING INVENTORY

Craig was back at the ship in the control room. He was a little confused. "Ship, what am I supposed to do now?"

"I can no longer advise you as to what. Once you have received your training to be Captain, you are to make decisions. I can impart all of the knowledge of mankind, but my programming cannot provide decisions."

"Lot of help you are." Craig sat at the console that was made to look like a standard computer console. He found that a good way to make decisions was sometimes to write down all of the ideas and then study them. He wrote them on a conventional computer keyboard and looked at them on the twenty inch monitor.

1. Mission is to save the Earth.

2. The only way is to get people off the Earth and into space to colonize other worlds.

3. Ship can make anything I can think of out of thin air, no out of nuclear fusion. Ten people could never ask for more than the computer could provide in terms of personal food, clothing, weapons, anything. Ship

cannot build another ship because that would require more energy than Ship can produce all at once. Therefore humans must build more ships.

4. The ship has the technology and the ability for me to impart that information to scientists, but science has to be able to put systems into production in quantity.

5. We need to get thousands into space for a decent gene pool. Even with crowding the ship could hold no more than one hundred people, besides ship will only allow one person, the Captain. After hundreds of generations and time running out, Ship has finally computed that the Captain should have a wife that can get on board. There is no possibility of getting more than the two on board? Multiple wives?

6. I have no credibility on Earth. I am only nineteen, soon to be twenty years old. My grades in college have been mediocre at best. I only have the knowledge and not the capability to produce even one major experiment, let alone a production line of space ships.

7. To that end, I am attempting to enlist the University of Oklahoma, its laboratories and political connections, to produce the scientific breakthroughs required to launch an evacuation into space. Where no one would listen to a nobody, they will listen to a University that has done laboratory testing. The University of Oklahoma has more CEOs, Chief Executive Officers, of top 1000 companies than any other non-private university. Those CEOs could be contacted by the University to get the new breakthroughs into production.

8. To get the money and resources required means my personally getting respect. To do that I am blackmailing the university into granting me a Ph.D. in exchange for helping them in their new developments.

a. A new lightweight super insulating, super strong, metal alloy.

b. A new drug in the war on AIDS.

c. A new airship design that almost eliminates aerodynamic drag.

d. A mathematics breakthrough that should help in interstellar navigation.

e. I prevented a nuclear attack on Israel.

f. I popped into the office of the President of the United States,

9. I have a week to wait before getting that Ph.D. and a month before my meeting with President Williams and his advisors. I don't need money when Ship can provide anything, including green backs.

10. Because of the shortness of time I must find a wife or help-mate quickly. That person must possess the following characteristics:

a. Looks. She must be very attractive and sexy.

b. She must have the overall physic to be healthy and strong. This changes the current concept of sexy somewhat. Since Twiggy became a hit model, and with the advent of television that makes people look fatter, skinny has been in. What look like slim sleek legs on television look like pencils in person. The physical features I am looking for are.

(1) Full breasted.

(2) Narrow waisted, female hormones at work, but not completely flat bellied. No fat, just not too skinny in the lower abdomen like a man is. A wide waist may indicate the presence of male hormones or not enough female hormones.

(3) Actually, the old Jayne Mansfield, Marilyn Monroe type. Not Twiggy or Dolly Pardon, but somewhere between. Maybe more like Brooke Shields but shorter since I am only five ten.

(4) Intelligence. Should have been listed number one, but the looks are critical and easier to spot. If she doesn't look like a girl I would want to take to bed, I don't care how smart she is. She must be very intelligent.

(5) Interests. She must be interested not only in things that will make for a good marriage, but will be of help in the mission. She must be interested is saving Earth through technology, but not the Einstein type of brainy.

(6) Height. Between five four and five seven. She needed to be at least average height since they might someday have ancestors on a strange planet living like settlers without technology. Craig did not want a girl too much taller than he was when she wore high heels.

11. Girls I have met and their pluses or minuses.

a. Dawn, Delta Delta, or Tri-Delt Sorority.

(1) Very nice build. Fits the model perfectly. Muscular. Muscles show, but not steroid male type muscles.

(2) Prudish?

(3) I know nothing about her.

b. Jill

(1) Also has a nice build. Not quite a busty as Dawn, but still nice. She has a smooth non muscled body.

(2) Sexy. Apparently a tease but not a slut. Into heavy petting. Not morally bound to having sex, but afraid of consequences.

(3) I know nothing about her.

d. The blond in the dorm.

(1) Nice body. Fits the model perfectly. Very physically fit. Blond. Blue eyes. I could love her.

(2) Virgin. Saving for a husband, but turned on by invisible man in the nude.

(3) Sleeps in the nude.

(4) From her books and picture album she could be smart enough. Seems interested and interesting, but don't know her well enough yet.

8 JILL AND DAWN

Craig was taking a shower back in his dorm room when suddenly he found himself standing on the sand down by the South Canadian river south of the campus. A nearly naked girl was running from some guy chasing her. Craig intercepted the guy and hit him with his best down field tackle he had learned playing football in high school. The guy, caught totally unaware was flattened into the sand. Craig rolled away. The girl was still running. The guy jumped up looking for blood, but couldn't see Craig. Craig picked up a piece of driftwood and clubbed him right in the face as he turned his direction. Craig could not identify either of them, but could see the girl was in trouble. The girl was hesitantly walking his direction.

Then Craig recognized the naked girl in the moonlight as Dawn, the first girl he approached after finding Ship. Craig was not sure how he got here or why.

As he wondered, the answer came into his head from the ship. *"You told Dawn that you would be her guardian angel. I was not sure whether to transport you to her aid, but then when she was obviously in trouble, I did transport you."*

Dawn had stopped twenty feet away, not sure what to do. Craig walked to her and put his arms around her. He felt her cold skin covered with sand and she felt his wetness from the shower mixed with the cold night air. Dawn jumped away from him. She said, "No. Not with him and not with you even if you are my guardian angel."

Craig said, "That's not a very nice way to talk after I saved you. I did save you didn't I?"

"Yes. He grabbed me in the parking lot at my sorority house and hit me. When I came to, we were driving out here on the river bed. I jumped out and ran. I discovered it hurt to run barefoot on the rocks and he caught me and started tearing my clothes off. I kicked him in the face and got away from him again, but he caught me again and tore off the rest of my clothing before I could get away again. Then I heard a thud and when I looked he had fallen down then I saw him get hit with a piece of driftwood, but couldn't see anyone else. I thought it might be you. Where were you? Hiding in his vehicle? That was the same guy you hit the other night. He must have been stalking me."

"No. I was taking a shower in my dorm room and suddenly found myself here on the riverbank."

"That doesn't make sense. Prove it."

Craig felt himself and could feel shampoo in his hair. He appeared in front of her.

Dawn said, "You're naked."

"No. I mean yes, but I just wanted to prove I was a person and I still have shampoo in my hair."

Dawn, being tired of running and knowing that she had been saved, did not back off as he approached her and put his arms around her. She said, "He might have been too big for me to handle, but I do know Judo and I'll break your arm if you try to harm me."

He offered her the top of his head. She felt it and took some suds to study in the moonlight. She said, "Aren't you cold?"

Craig replied, "Now that you mention it. I am freezing. Where is his vehicle?"

"I'm freezing too. Back that way."

Craig put his arm around her and they walked together for warmth and comfort together as Craig let her lead him to the guy's vehicle. He opened the door for her and then asked, "Where are the keys?"

Dawn said, "Whoops. When I jumped out of the door, I grabbed his keys and threw them over in that underbrush somewhere. Here is a blanket I found over me when I came to in this car. We'd better share it."

Craig moved over to the passenger seat and they locked the doors in case the guy came to and came back. As they huddled naked together under the blanket for warmth, Craig tried to talk to her, but she started crying with big sobs and clinging to him. Craig zapped them back to her sorority room where it was warmer. They appeared on her bed and he leaned them backwards so that they were both lying on her bed. The lights were out and Dawn didn't realize that they were no longer in the Chevy Blazer. Her sobbing gradually subsided. Her breathing gradually became normal

Dawn said, "I'm getting warm now. I hope you don't mind me using you for body heat."

Craig said, "I'm all yours."

"Who are you anyway?"

"I'm a college student here. You will probably hear of me by the end of the week so I'll tell you if you keep it a secret, I'm Craig Decker."

"Pleased to formally meet you, Craig Decker. Now what were you doing out on the riverbank naked with soap on your hair in the moonlight." With that she raised up to look at him better and opened her eyes. "How did we get here?"

Craig said, "I told you I have powers. I really was in the shower when I found myself watching you being chased on the river bank. It was cold in the Blazer so I zapped us to your room."

About that time Dawn apparently realized that they were naked together on her bed and moved away from him, "No. I don't care who you are, I am not going to have sex with you."

Craig let her get up holding the blanket to hide herself. "Can I come back and talk with you?"

Dawn said, "I do owe you that much, but not now and not naked."

Craig said, "Okay. Later. Call the police on that guy with the Chevy Blazer." and zapped away.

…………..

Craig decided to spend a day or so around Jill to find out about both her and Dawn. He couldn't help but think that a lot of apparently random things happen for reasons. He needed to find out if there was any reason that he had run into these girls.

It was nine o'clock on Saturday morning when he went to Jill's room. She was sleeping. He was in invisible mode when he arrived and stayed that way as he rummaged through her room looking for clues on her interests and studies in college. He found a grade report from the first semester. She had taken nineteen hours which is a heavy load for a sophomore at the University of Oklahoma and a Sorority member. Last semester she had taken anthropology, physics, chemistry, zoology, and mathematics 201. Her overall grade point average was an impressive three point four. Her birthday was in September so she would not turn twenty until starting her junior year of college. Her major was petrochemical engineering. "I never would have believed it of Jill. She's a brain with technical interests. Maybe Dawn ran into me so I would meet Jill. She may not be muscled, but that has not been as important for women since pioneer times, men either, as far as that goes."

Craig decided that he really wanted to talk with Jill, not go to bed with her like she wanted. If he appeared to her, he would just be a strange man in her room. If he was invisible, she would probably go for him physically. The idea was to figure out how to get her alone to talk. He got her phone number off the telephone and then reappeared back in his dorm room and called her.

"Jill?"

"Yes. Who's this?"

"Craig Decker. You don't really know me, but we met through Dawn."

"Hah. Dawn hasn't had a boyfriend since she's been here at college and I met her when she was in rush."

"Now did I say I was a boyfriend? Maybe I should have said male friend of Dawn's. She introduced us once. At any rate, I was hoping that I could take you to dinner and interview you for a class I am taking."

"I like your voice. Sounds familiar. Have we met?

"Not really, but I have seen you before at your sorority house when I was with Dawn.

"I don't remember Dawn having a boy here. Interview me for what class?"

"How about I interview you first and then tell you what class? That way I won't spoil the interview by telling you in advance. Okay?"

"Oh well, like when?"

"Like now?

"You must be putting me on. I have a date tonight for a party at the SAE house."

"How about lunch at the Main Street Brewing Company and I'll take you to dinner some evening at your convenience to pay you back for the interview?"

What kind of car do you drive?"

"What kind do you like?"

"Fast."

"How about a red Dodge Viper?"

"Is that like a Dodge Stealth?"

"No. A Viper is a two seat convertible with a ten cylinder engine. The fastest production car made in the United States."

"Cool. I'll be looking for a small red convertible."

"How about eleven so we can get a quiet seat?"

"Make it eleven-thirty."

Jill thought to herself, "This is probably the worst idea in a long time. Maybe I should call Dawn and ask about him? I shouldn't really go out with a guy I don't know. What if he is a creep? If Dawn knows him and introduced us, he must be okay. Dawn doesn't know very many guys. If he has a Dodge Viper or whatever, he must have some money."

Jill studied for awhile and then started getting ready for the date. She had not had very many dates in the daytime. This was a first to have a formal lunch date. She had gone for lunch with a lot of guys, but they had not called her, picked her up, and taken her just like an evening date. Of course it was for an interview, but still, he had asked her out for lunch and surely a lunch date could not get too serious. She went to her closet and went through her clothes trying to find just the right thing. "I can always just not come outside if I don't see a car I like when eleven thirty comes. No, that's an evening dress. This one looks like church. Jeans and a crop top? Hmmm," she said to herself, "this white tennis skirt and white blousy crop top would look sexy and acceptable for lunch at the Brewers. Besides, I can always get a ride home with someone else if he's a creep. I'll probably know someone there anyway. Okay."

Jill went into her bathroom and took thirty minutes fixing her hair and making sure that her makeup was just right. She chose a pale blue eye shadow to accentuate her blue eyes, black mascara, and a hot pink lip gloss, put on with a brush. When right she put on the tennis skirt and crop top and then stood in front of the mirror. "Looks like I just came from a tennis match." She added white tennis shoes with no socks and then realized it was time. When she looked out the window she saw the sexiest red two seater sports car she had ever seen with chrome exposed exhaust pipes on the sides under the diminutive doors.

She was impressed when she bounced out the door to admire the car. She said, "Craig?"

"How many other red Dodge Vipers are there on campus?"

"This is the first I remember seeing. I've seen them on television before." They made small talk about the weather and the car until they got into Brewers. When they were seated at a quiet corner reserved for Craig at the back corner of Brewers Craig started his interview.

"I'm sorry Jill; I missed your last name?"

"Jill McClendon. What's your last name?"

"Decker. McClendon has a nice ring to it."

The waiter came, they ordered, and Craig went right to the questions, "Shall we get right to the interview. Some of my questions are pretty strange, but don't laugh. They are serious questions. Your answers are very important to me. Question one. How do you feel about the space program?"

"Too slow. The space station should have been up ten years before. There is so much research we could have done if we had the station then. In addition they keep phasing it back making it smaller and simpler. MIR was never anything except a space condo, not a real science station."

"Okay. Do you feel like mankind will or should someday make it to other solar systems?"

Jill said, "From what I understand about space and distance, the astronauts could not live long enough to make it to the nearest star."

Craig said, "What if the spaceship could accelerate to faster than the speed of light?"

Jill said, "In the first place, we both know that is impossible. Matter changes to energy at the speed of light. If a ship were to hit the speed of light it would be one big explosion."

Craig said, "This is just a what if. You are quoting Einstein's equation Energy equals Mass times Speed or C squared? What about the inverse, Mass equals C squared divided by Energy. Actually that is not it, but the idea is that the mass of the space ship becomes infinite as the speed approaches the speed of light." Craig was playing dumb.

Jill said, "You're right, the formulas wrong, but I am familiar with it."

"Okay, if the space ship mass is infinite then it must be approaching the mass of our galaxy. Then the passengers in that ship are also infinite. What if size as well as mass were increased to near infinite size. Well then, imagine that by walking from the back of the ship near Earth to the front, the passenger has walked from Earth to the other side of the galaxy. I'm just saying that if man could quickly travel from one star to another in hours or days instead of years, then would you be for man traveling and settling planets around other stars?"

Jill said, "Just for what its worth, which is, not much, if travel were anywhere near that fast, then, yes, I would be all for exploring the stars."

"Would you be interested in colonizing another planet, if that were possible and a planet could be found with an Earth climate?"

Jill said, "I'm not sure. I would not want to be the one of the first, but after civilization were established I would like to go visit. No, I might be persuaded to be an early settler if the conditions were not too bleak. It would depend. I think I would like the adventure"

"What if, just for what if's sake, the Earth were going to be destroyed in ten years, would you then work to be one of the few thousand to be evacuated to space to colonize other planets for mankind's survival?"

Jill said, "Under those circumstances, of course I would want to be one of the survivors. Who wouldn't want to be one of them?"

"What if a planet had not been found and mankind was just going to space in ships? Of course those ships would be self supporting and could keep the crew alive for generations if necessary."

Jill moved around the table to sit beside Craig. "Yes, I still would go. You didn't answer why most people would not want to go."

Craig said, "You would be surprised how many would not believe the danger or would not want to take the chance of leaving even when destruction were assured. Remember the story of Noah's Ark? There is evidence there was such a flood. The people laughed at Noah."

"I guess you're right. You think you can get man into space, and you can disappear, right? You're not so bad; you can come visit me anytime if you can get into my room without being seen. If you know what I mean."

Craig did not acknowledge this invitation. She put her hand in his lap which he instantly responded to. Jill said, "Yep. You're him aren't you? What are these ships going to use for fuel? How are they going to get free of Earth's gravity?"

Craig had not considered fuel. Pretty stupid of him. Mankind could never master the nuclear capability of his ship in the time available. They would need some other form of fuel. Maybe Jill was the right one to become his wife and join him on the mission to get man into space. She had appeared to be a nymphomaniac, but from what Dawn and Jill both said, she was a tease that liked heavy petting, but would not submit to sex with a man out of fear of disease or an unwanted pregnancy. They had finished their meal. Craig asked, "Can you spend the rest of the day with me to answer a few more questions?"

"You're not him. The invisible one, are you. No, I told you I have a date tonight. It doesn't matter that I don't really know the guy I'm going to the party with. I don't stand people up. I need several hours to get ready."

Craig put sufficient money on the table and they went back to his car. Norman is a small town and it only took moments to drive Jill back to her sorority house. He let her off, disappointed that he had not been able to spend the day and evening with her.

Jill said, "Come by and visit me after midnight, if you can make yourself invisible, okay?"

"Maybe."

"Ha. Nice talking with you, maybe next time I won't have another date to go on."

"Yeah, maybe."

Craig decided that he should look in on one of the other girls he had met to find out more about them. Craig went down the short list of only three girls he had met since this began. Only Dawn was in her room. Craig went to her room and appeared in her room in person. He sat on the edge of her bed. She was sitting at her desk, studying her textbooks. He said, "Dawn?"

She started and looked in his direction. "You're back and not even invisible." She turned her body ninety degrees to see him better.

"No need. You have already seen me. I came by to ask you some questions."

"Anything you want. I owe you my life. I'm afraid I still don't look like much, but I'm perfectly okay. I'm the one that would like to be invisible."

Craig looked at her in her negligee. It was semi-transparent lace. She had on the traditional bikini panties that came to her waist at the sides and dipped low in front. Her hips were almost completely bare. In fact the negligee did not really cover her from the waist down because it had hiked up to her waist as she lay on her side reading. The sun from the window came through her negligee, she was full busted. She had some bruises on her legs and wrists, but it was mainly her face that was now turning more green and yellow versus black and blue. It looked like it hurt. He could remember that her face was very attractive, but you couldn't tell right now.

"You're gorgeous. Question one. How do you feel about the space program?"

"Very intriguing. It is frustrating that the government won't put more emphasis on it. We should already have permanent stations on the Moon and Mars. What if no one had explored anywhere? The only places left are the ocean and space. The ocean is as hostile as space. A space ship, once in space has to be strong enough to maintain fourteen pounds or less of air. A submarine has to withstand many atmospheres of pressure. People cannot breathe water any better than trying to breath space. We have the technology to fly into space from an airport, but where is the National Aerospace Plane or NASP? It would only take a little more to achieve orbit. If we could cheaply achieve orbit we could cheaply build a space station. If we could cheaply build a large space station we could more cheaply move further."

"Okay. Do you feel like mankind will or should someday make it to other solar systems?"

Dawn said, "We are a long way from that. We need to explore our own solar system first. To travel to the stars would mean building huge ships in space that could support generations of people because the astronauts could not live long enough to make it to the nearest star."

Craig said, "What if the spaceship could accelerate to faster than the speed of light?"

Dawn said, "Impossible. Unless you know something I don't know. Matter changes to energy at the speed of light. If a ship were to hit the speed of light it would be one big explosion."

Craig said, "You know Einstein's equation Energy equals Mass times Speed or C squared? What about the inverse, the idea is that the mass of the space ship becomes infinite as the speed approaches the speed of light."

Dawn said, "You mean like Star Trek when they fly at warp nine. That would be neat. If the space ship mass is infinite then it must also approach infinity. Then the passengers in that ship are also infinite."

"You're on the right track. I'm just saying that if man could quickly travel from one star to another in hours or days or at least weeks or months instead of years, then would you be for man traveling and settling planets around other stars?"

Dawn said, "Of course. That's what I said; man needs to be out exploring the stars."

"Then you would be interested in colonizing another planet, if that was possible and a planet could be found with an Earth climate?"

Dawn said, "Absolutely. Think what we could learn. If God allowed us into space at all, and since he has allowed travel to the Moon and robots to reach Mars, then God intends for us to spread our civilization to he stars."

"What if the Earth were going to be destroyed in ten years, would you then work to be one of the few thousand to be evacuated to space to colonize other planets for mankind's survival?"

Dawn said, "I would work to get any human into space. If I could be one of them, fine. If not, then I would be able to help mankind. Are you asking me all those questions because I am majoring in astrophysics and aeronautical engineering?"

"No, I didn't know that was what you were majoring in. What if a planet had not been found and mankind was just going to space in ships? Of course those ships would be self supporting and could keep the crew alive for generations if necessary."

Dawn moved from the desk to sit beside Craig on the bed. "Yes, I would still go if I were one of the privileged few. Once we had a cheap air and space craft to take off from Earth and fly into lower space and then use rockets to boost into space. Once free of gravity, we could use ion or nuclear propulsion to maintain constant acceleration to provide some gravity until half way there and then deceleration the rest of the way. But an engine with the power to accelerate to the speed of light would require constant nuclear explosions which would contaminate space, but there is a lot of space."

"Sounds like you have a lot of it worked out."

"No, scientists before me have that all figured out. I just read a lot."

"I, uh, ran into you in the gym and know you are in to physical conditioning. What about sex?"

"I owe you my life. I guess it's okay if you want to." She sat up on the side of the bed and started to undo her negligee."

"No. I don't mean now. I mean, how do you feel about sex and children and so forth."

"You mean you don't want to." She tied her negligee back in place. "I think sex has its place, I just haven't had the time. I want to be in love when I have sex."

"Thank you for the interview, Dawn."

"Before you go. Why did you ask me such strange questions?"

"I shouldn't tell you. I won't tell you that. Ah. I plan to get man into space within ten years. I don't mean a Mar's station. I mean other planets. You'll know it all eventually. The new metal I gave the university and the new aerodynamic shape are both suited to go into space. The strength of the metal means that small meteoroids will not damage it at super speeds. It is a near perfect insulator meaning minimal energy required for heating or cooling. The weight and the aerodynamics mean a maximum payload going into space at minimal energy expended. A single jet engine off of a commuter jet out take an aircraft larger than the shuttle into the upper reaches of the atmosphere where a rocket engine for a small communications satellite would be sufficient to boost it past the moon, except for payload. It still takes a certain amount of thrust to accelerate a certain mass to a certain speed."

"You're right, if that new metal is as light and strong as you say and if the aerodynamics of your model is really that good, then it will be a major breakthrough. However, it may take years to get your new alloy into production. What can I do to help?"

Craig said, "I don't know yet. If you have any additional ideas, let me know. Well, it's well past dinner time. Can I take you somewhere to eat?"

"No. I ate early and I can pick up snacks in the kitchen. I don't plan on showing my face for at least a week. I've arranged to get notes on my classes from others. I don't want anyone to see me like this."

"Well, I'm going out to eat. See you."

…………

Craig disappeared to his dorm room and then went down to his Dodge Viper given him by the ship. He drove down to the Interurban restaurant for a good steak. He had been forgetting to eat three meals a day. He sat back and just watched the people in the restaurant. No pretty girls except for a couple of waitresses. One came to his table to take his order.

Craig asked her, "Student at OU?"

"Yes."

"Me too. What's your major?"

"Mathematics."

"Are you going to be a math teacher?"

"Yes, if I make it through school. Are you ready to order?" She had a nice body and a pretty face, but Craig already had three girls to consider. He wrote her name down on a napkin to remember as a backup. Craig ordered and she left. Her name tag said Sally Carmen. He pondered the girls. He was also concerned about her exaggerated figure possibly being a health problem.

9 CRIME WAVE

Craig had the Iranian leader zapped into the federal prison at Leavenworth, Kansas and then put messages on the prison computers telling who and where he was. He also left a message on the President's desk in the oval office in the Whitehouse. He had the ship leave a message about his incarceration on all of the desks of all of the questionable leaders of the world to show them that anyone can be arrested regardless of the security. It was only hours before the news hits the streets. Iran denied it but found that their leader had disappeared out of his bomb proof secret bunker under the noses of his personal guard. No one except Craig knew how he had arrived in prison.

Craig went back to his ship and got an update on world news. He winked into the Kremlin and wandered around some. He sat in with some of the leaders of the remains of the Soviet Union. He wasn't sure what to do about the territorial battles between the Soviet Union and its old states. He could see both sides of the argument and was not sure that he should intervene at this time. There might be more important issues.

One thing that stood out in U.S. news was crime. Craig felt that for the United States to lead humankind into space in the space of ten years, he needed to control some other things. The economy was relatively strong. The balance of payments was not good, but going down to the lowest in years. Imports of automobiles were not that bad now. American's had learned that American cars were the better deal. You could get more for the money and the hidden service costs of Japanese cars had been made public. Most people knew that the cost of routine service for a Japanese car had exceeded the cost of increased repairs. His new metal would be impossible to duplicate without the formula and with the new metal the United States automobiles would be made of soon. Small parts and electronics had moved almost entirely overseas because of labor costs. He would have to sit in the economics learning lesson on Ship to decide what to do.

The United States had a crime epidemic. The growth of street gangs made many cities, even the suburbs, unsafe after dark. He could not patrol everywhere of course. No one would listen to him in law enforcement. He was just another teenager to them. At least for now.

A lot of the crime seemed to be drug related. Making it legal would be stupid. There were already plenty of suppliers in the United States. Some inner city kids were on a semi-permanent high with no knowledge of right and wrong. According to the ship, thirty percent of the youth of the United States between the ages of twelve and nineteen were high on some form of drug or alcohol over fifty percent of the time. They had no respect for their own lives and therefore no respect for the welfare of others. There had always been gang activity, even in small town America. The difference was that in the forties, fifties, sixties, and seventies, gangs used physical strength to fight each other. Their weapons were fists occasionally augmented with chains or baseball bats to injure people. Some schools had fights before, after or during games, but this was different. Now someone just walked into a room with an UZI, or drove past with a shotgun trying to kill people. It was one thing to meet and shout at each other or leave each other with bruises, but killing had crept in during the later eighties. Standard school fights were out. Now people were gunned down in the hallways or on the school grounds. Why? Drugs.

Craig studied the drug situation. Drugs were available everywhere, but the main source for the United States was from South America. Colombia was a major supplier, but Uruguay had become a major supplier, especially for large shipments of the cheap stuff. Craig had an advantage in that the nothing on the Earth could be hidden from the ship. He decided to have the ship monitor all ships being loaded in Colombian aircraft from Uruguay for Cocaine products and stop those ships and aircraft from reaching the United States. What he discovered that every ship out of Colombia that would go to the United States before returning to its home had Cocaine on board as did most of the aircraft.

Ship reminded him that the fighter could go underwater slower but incredibly fast. The aerodynamics worked underwater as well although the light weight meant using power to stay under water because the metal of the ship was lighter than water.

Craig took the fighter under water as they came into American waters and melted down the propellers to where the engines vibrated so badly that the ships had to call for help from the Coast Guard. Craig also placed a call to the Coast Guard to tell them where to find the cocaine on board. With aircraft Craig flew up under them and melted their gear doors just enough to keep the gear doors from opening on landing. That restricted the aircraft to landing at bigger airports where they could foam the runways. By Friday, over six thousand nine hundred tons of cocaine had been seized. A lot still came in by truck across the border, but prices were sky rocketing.

Just in case he was found out by organized crime, he had the ship place his family under watch. The ship would not zip them to the ship, but it could blink them into a police station if anyone tried to do them harm. Craig didn't figure that organized crime would be able to identify him because he used a voice changer when calling the Coast Guard when he called from his fighter.

....

Craig attended the meeting in the office of the president of the University of Oklahoma. Professor Myrtle and Professor Davis were not there because Craig's new alloy and his wind tunnel model were both in testing with the Professor's accompanying the testing. They both had written glowing letters as well as informing the university president of what was happening.

....

The military had attempted to copy the model in aluminum and composite fibers, but were not able to duplicate the effect because of the relative weakness of their materials, but the improvement in aerodynamics were many times the previous best efforts. Craig's model was phenomenal. The model was so light weight compared to their copies that it practically floated.

The new metal alloy had been through everything known in the laboratories with no damage of any kind. It was impervious to anything they had including high pressure diamond drills. It was actually lighter than Styrofoam for its size and far stronger and harder than anything known. Professor Myrtle refused to give up the formula and the metal was so impervious that the labs had no way to analyze it. Professor Myrtle did explain how it acted as it cooled and how it was shaped.

The mathematics professor was still rambling on about the possible ramifications of the formula that Craig had written on his blackboard. He had the formula tested through super computers many times and it appeared correct, but might take a hundred years to prove.

Professor Gimble was more positive still. In Petri dishes the new serum seemed to kill the aids virus instantly on contact with no harm to healthy tissue. Rats infected with HIV were now testing HIV free. At the University of Oklahoma Medical Hospital in Oklahoma City, three AIDS patients expected to die in days were now testing HIV free, but warned that it may only be in remission. They would need to wait five years or more for FDA approval. Some rats that had been apparently cured by the new anti-virus had received total transfusions with HIV infected blood. The rats HIV was still in the blood, but apparently only dead virus within twenty-four hours even without a booster shot. Within sixty hours the rats were HIV free. If the testing bore out the original testing and if the FDA approved it then the virus could be given to almost anyone that had active HIV and those people might not only be cured, but may have a permanent immunity. So far, the rats and people had not died of the serum just as Craig said they would not. The jury is still out of course. I vote for giving him a doctorate in biomedical research if he will work with us.

The math professor argued that he should be able to get equal time. Craig was awarded doctorate degrees in Aeronautical Engineering, Metallurgy, biochemistry, and Mathematics. These were not honorary degrees but full fledged "awarded through testing" degrees.

Craig showed the mathematics department how to test his formula better and gave them some new formulas for interstellar navigation. He worked with biochemistry on methods for mass production of the serum but warned again, that there would be a percentage of fatalities from the virus and that it should never be given to someone with a chance of recovery.

After a week of perfecting the production techniques, Craig said, "I have a formula for a serum to provide immunity to HIV for people not yet infected that is both one hundred percent effective and one hundred percent safe, but first I will have to find the time for the chemical industry to make some advances for required for the serum."

Professor Gimble promised to make an appointment with his for the following week with the chemistry department. Craig said, "Professor Gimble, I need to take a week off. Things have been happening very fast and I need the time to think review where chemistry is today and how to get where we want to go."

Professor Gimble said, "Of course **Doctor** Decker. You have worked wonders here in the past two weeks. You haven't mentioned what kind of salary or grant you are looking for."

Craig said, "Money is literally not the object. If you want to put me down for a salary or grant, use it for your research. I have everything I need except the breakthroughs I need. By the way, I am not interested in a cure for AIDS, but the cure for AIDS leads to the vaccine and the vaccine against AIDS works as a vaccine against most cancers."

Professor Gimble said, "A vaccine against cancer. Craig, I mean doctor, do you realize what that would mean to the world."

"My theory is that AIDS is the result of the HIV virus that breaks down the immune system. Cancer is the result of the body fighting a virus too hard. Sometimes the body cells are weakened by a carcinogen and they turn cancerous when fighting some common virus. Lung cancer is weakened lung cells fighting off a rhino virus to the point of reproducing too fast. The weakened cells need more blood to supply the cells with food to fight and these in turn cause growths of tissue that develop into cancer. This vaccine will prevent any harmful virus from living in the body including what we sometimes call the common cold and flu. No. It won't cure the common cold, but it will reduce its incidence tremendously. There are still allergies that can develop into sinus infections and pneumonia. I suspect there are more allergy related sicknesses than the common cold."

"No. It will not cure cancer only prevent many forms of it. The cancer prevented includes lung cancer, throat cancer, intestinal and stomach cancer, and colon cancer. It will not prevent skin cancer, cirrhosis of the liver from drinking, kidney cancer, brain cancer, and many others. It will reduce the incidence of these cancers by forty to fifty percent, but it won't eliminate them and will not cure cancer already active. Bone cancer is one hundred percent preventable and can be reduced by this serum. Bone cancer is caused by the production of white blood cells to fight virus and other cancer. Once the virus is gone permanently, many cancers already started will slow, but especially bone."

"HIV is a particularly virulent virus that causes a weak body to wither and die, sometimes by cancer. The first serum that you already have will kill HIV, but full blown AIDS is the inability of the body to fight anymore. A person with a good diet and exercise program that stays away from unhealthy things might survive for many years but a weak homosexual with a poor diet and no spirit of survival will die quickly from the HIV. The second serum, not yet possible prevents all harmful viruses, including HIV."

....

Craig left to make some additional war on illegal drugs. He again disabled ships at sea smuggling drugs and ruined the tires on the aircraft. He really was tired because while the ships were slow, he was spending his nights tracking aircraft. Many were getting through during the hours he worked on the serum and slept and ate. There weren't so many ships because so many had been disabled and then impounded. The aircraft drug traffic had been reduced by eighty percent because of damaged then impounded aircraft. Craig could not figure out how to stop the truck traffic.

The only way to fight the drug traffic was to get the management that ordered the trade and got the profit. The smallest number were the drug lords of South America. Craig spent hours producing video tapes of evidence where Ship had monitored and recorded the incriminating activities of the biggest drug lords. Craig had the ship transport twenty of the biggest South American dealers to jails in Colombia, Uruguay, and the United States. One minute they were in their fortresses and suddenly they were behind bars. Simultaneously with their transport the video tapes showed up in the hands of the prosecution along with the prison location of the perpetrator. It took nearly an hour per dealer.

Craig was exhausted to the point of not being able to think straight. He slept for six hours straight and like most young men, woke horny. A healthy young man of nineteen doesn't need but four hours a night plus a nap here and there. He had slept six hours.

Craig had not forgotten his quest to find a mate to join him in his mission and he desperately needed help that had access to the ships pow

10 CHEERLEADER

There was one girl that Craig had not talked with now that might be available, the cheerleader he had always admired. She appeared to be taken, but did not know that for sure. He had sat around so long at the restaurant that it was already ten when he got back to his dorm room. He asked the ship where she was and ship told him she was in her room. He blinked to her room. She was in bed asleep. He was unsure as to whether to wake her or leave. Instead, he watched her. It was not dark in the room. She had left the bathroom light on and there was a street light outside that was unblocked. She had her blinds wide open. She looked real good at the football games.

He had ship zap him a fine point flashlight and he inspected her text books, pictures, and letters from home. She slept. He decided to wake her up and ask his questions like he had been asking the others. He pulled her covers toward the foot of the bed. She pulled them back. While she was pulling, he pulled back. She sat up and looked. She turned on her bedside light and looked for a moment went to the windows to close the blinds then across the room to the light switch and turned on the overhead lights. She put the covers back on the bed.

Craig said softly, "Dreaming?"

She quickly spun around and looked toward his voice. Craig said, "Dream. It's only a dream."

She was obviously confused. She had been asleep. Now she heard his voice, but could see no person. She said, "Is someone there?"

Craig replied, "Only your imagination." She went toward his voice. Craig didn't move out of her path, but let her bump into him. She froze almost against him. She had hit his leg with her hand and was now standing within inches. She could feel him. She was maybe five foot six. She could hear his breathing. He could feel her warmth. She was breathing very shallow. She reached out and touched his waist with one hand and then explored a few inches down until she hit the top button on his Levi's. He was not wearing a belt. She quickly moved her hand away and then reached out a few inches higher. Craig said, "Imagination is running away?"

She explored up feeling his sweat shirt. "I must be asleep." She was startled by her own voice.

Craig replied, "Must be asleep. Don't panic. Go with the flow. Relax. Might was well go back to bed."

She did. Craig turned off the overhead light as she lay down on the bed. She said, "Is someone there?"

Craig replied, "An active imagination? Shouldn't be alone in your room on a Saturday night. You really wanted to go out. Right?"

"Wrong. I choose to be alone."

Craig walked up beside the bed where she was stiffly on her back. He turned out the bedside light. She probably would have screamed, but there was no one else in the sorority house. He sat on the edge of her bed. Craig said, "Remember, you're not afraid of being alone. I only want you to explore your inner self in this dream."

"I'm not dreaming."

"If not. Then what is your name?"

"Shelby Denton."

"Explore these rather strange questions and relax. Question one. How do you feel about the space program?"

"What?"

Craig repeated, "How do you feel about the space program."

Shelby said, "This is crazy. Okay, I'll play along. Are you an extraterrestrial come to abduct me?"

"No. I'm not from space. I'm human and a student at OU. The question was how do you feel about the space program?

Shelby said, "It has provided a lot of new technology. It has ushered in the computer age, but it hasn't done much in years now."

"Okay. Do you feel like mankind will or should someday make it to other solar systems?"

Shelby said, "Only if we can find some faster way of getting there."

Craig said, "What if the spaceship could accelerate to faster than the speed of light?"

Shelby said, "As in Star Trek. That has always been my favorite show. Yes, of course mankind should explore."

"Would you be interested in colonizing another planet, if that were possible and a planet could be found with an Earth climate?"

Shelby said, "I think I would like the adventure"

"What if, just for what ifs sake, the Earth was going to be destroyed in ten years, would you then work to be one of the few thousand to be evacuated to space to colonize other planets for mankind's survival?"

Shelby said, "Under those circumstances, of course."

"What if a planet had not been found and mankind was just going to space in ships? Of course those ships would be self supporting and could keep the crew alive for generations if necessary."

"I'm not sure."

Craig said, "I want to get man into space. You will hear about me soon, I hope."

Shelby reached out for him and grabbed his sleeve. "You are real, but I can't see you. Why?"

"Because I am invisible. I have gained some special capabilities recently. I do not want to be identified."

Shelby said, "Why did you come to my room? How did you know I would be alone in the house? What are you going to do to me?"

"I'm not here to hurt you in any way. I came here because you are very intriguing to me. I have always admired you as a cheerleader. You not only were more precise, but your legs were so straight."

"What?"

"The other cheerleaders have bowed legs or are so muscled that their muscles prevent their legs from fitting together nicely. Your legs were so beautifully formed. Your moves so perfect. I followed you home Friday after your practice. I saw that you had books of science fiction, but I also saw that picture of the boy and his family. I presume he is a serious boyfriend or fiancée from how you look at him in the picture."

"My family and my brother."

"You don't have a steady boyfriend?"

"No."

"Why aren't you out with the rest of your sorority?"

"My only experience with sex was not very good. I thought I was in love and he in love with me. I did it with him. He banged me a few times which hurt like hell and left. He dropped me after having spent fifteen minutes in a motel. He literally left me there crying in the bed. I had to call a girlfriend to give me a ride home. I read a lot and not all of it is non-fiction. I have read about how sex can be good. I would like to meet a man that really cared about me and have his children. I don't really know about sex. I have to get my education before I worry about sex. Once I have an established career, I can survive if my boyfriend or husband packs. The sorority puts up with my anti-social behavior because I am a third generation legacy in this sorority. I exercise to keep my figure and fix my face and hair out of my own pride, not to attract men. I've never told anyone, why am I telling you?"

"What if you were given the opportunity to be the most powerful woman in the world and be given more knowledge than any woman in history? Would you then look for a man?"

Shelby said, "Yes. I might. With you? No. I can't see you. I would never marry for power or wealth alone. I would have to like the person and feel attracted to him."

"Would you make it with me in exchange for this power and wealth?

"Absolutely not. I was cheapened once and that was enough. I am absolutely not for sale. Why are you here?"

"Good answer. I like that answer. If I were to prove to you that I can give you everything and prove that I can take you into space with me to explore other worlds, would you go with me?"

"That's a terrible question. Yes, I would like power and knowledge. Yes, I would love to go into space and explore new worlds, but I couldn't. I want to love and be loved. I don't know you. I don't even know if I'm awake or dreaming."

"Pretend you are dreaming. What is your major?

"Chemistry. Why?"

"Remember, this is only a dream." Craig left her to think.

It was past midnight. Craig decided to check in on Jill. She was just telling her date that she had to leave the party. Jill told her date, "I'm sorry. I'm not feeling well. Would you take me home?"

Jill didn't allow any side trips and only gave him a peck on the cheek before running for the front door of the house. She went straight to her room and asked, "Are you here?"

Craig was watching by virtual reality, but did not appear. He watched Jill feel around the room. She was disappointed. She said out loud, "Should have known that Craig fellow wasn't for real. He was taking me for a ride. He did have a nice car. When I asked my date tonight what a Dodge Viper was, he seemed very impressed. Oh well. I got a free lunch. Forget him."

Craig wanted to crawl into bed with her, but decided that he needed to keep things on an intellectual level where possible. By his not showing up, she would not believe Craig was the invisible guy.

Craig desperately wanted to find a mate. He knew that he needed months to make the choice and then the girls might not agree to be his mate. You can't be in love in a few days. He had to choose right or the ship would not accept her. He seemed to have several good choices already, but decided to zip around the country for a few days trying to select some more choices.

That was when Craig realized that he didn't have to do this by chance and he didn't need to be restricted to the University of Oklahoma. As a minimum, the University of Oklahoma would only be a temporary base and the ship or somewhere private in the world would be the long term base. No. That was wrong. The long term base would be on some other planet in some other solar system. His wife and help-mate would have to explore the galaxy looking for a home. He needed someone with good judgment. Education was not that important because the ship could make them experts in any field if they had intelligence.

The ship in fact could quickly give him any information on anyone in the world just by asking. Craig went to the ship to ask some questions. "Ship, I want the names of three girls that are intelligent with an IQ of at least 130 and potential interest in exploring the universe. They have to be what I would call attractive based on the girls I have found so far. Also she should be between five foot four and five foot seven and weigh between one hundred ten and one hundred twenty-five pounds. She should have a clear complexion and long hair. She should be healthy with a good genetic background for long life and good health with an ability to have multiple children with minimum trouble."

Craig figured to test his wish list, that he should give it a reality test by having the computer evaluate the girls he already knew something about. "Oh, Ship, before you tell me about girls, tell me which of the girls I am already considering meet those qualifications and tell me why the girls that don't meet those qualifications don't."

The computer made the following list.

1. Dawn. IQ one hundred thirty-five. Five foot six. One hundred twenty pounds. Percent of fat seven percent. Dense muscle mass. Has excellent complexion and long hair. Grand parents on both sides lived past eighty. Should have no serious health problems or problems with children. Pre-

disposed toward exploring space.

2. Jill. IQ one hundred forty-eight. Five foot four and a half. One hundred ten pounds. Percent of fat nine percent. Physically fit. Has excellent complexion and long hair. All grand parents lived past eighty. Should have no serious health problems or problems having children. Will go where husband goes, even into space or space colony.

3. Betty Sue. Unacceptable. You know her as first girl in dorm. IQ one hundred ten. Percent of fat twelve percent. Not physically fit. Oldest male grand parent died at sixty-eight from heart problems. Mother had breast cancer and died at forty-two. Genetic disposition to cancer and heart problems. Children would most likely need cesarean section. Would not be likely to stay with husband or go into space. Dislike and distrust of science.

4. Heather. You know her as second girl in dorm and virgin. IQ one hundred thirty-eight. Percent of fat eight percent. Physically fit. Has excellent complexion and long hair. Great grand parents lived past eighty. Grand parents still alive past eighty. Excellent health history. Large family where couples averaged seven children with no significant health problems. Wants space exploration. Would like to be settler in new area like previous generations.

6. Sarah. Unacceptable. Height five-foot three. Eighteen percent body fat, unacceptable physical fitness for new colony. Family history of problems with child bearing. Bone structure indicates problems with child bearing.

8. Shelby. Unacceptable. Short hair. Otherwise acceptable. IQ one hundred forty-two. Percent of fat seven point three. Physically fit. Excellent complexion Great great grand parents lived past ninety. One great grand parent lived to one hundred four. Grand parents still alive but not yet eighty. No health problems. Pregnancy should be very easy with natural child birth preferred under severe circumstances. Natural pioneer woman. Burning desire for personal space travel.

Girls you have not met yet.

1. Nanette Svorsky. IQ one hundred fifty-three. Body fat six percent. Five foot seven. One hundred twenty-five pounds of muscle. Very athletic. Excellent tanned complexion with no pre-disposition to cancer or other disease. Grand parents lived past eighty. Child bearing excellent. Desires personal travel to another planet.

2. Janeil O'Leary. IQ one hundred forty. Body fat eight percent. Five foot five. One hundred fifteen pounds. Physically fit. Child bearing excellent. College major astral physics.

3. Sandra (Sandy) Scoffield. IQ one hundred twenty-nine. Body fat eight percent. Five foot four. One hundred fifteen pounds. Very athletic. Excellent dark complexion. Excellent child bearing. Fan of Star Trek.

"Okay, Ship. Take me to number one." Craig appeared invisible in Nanette's apartment on the beach. She was a physical wonder. She was weight lifting. Even her breasts rippled with muscle. She had posters on the walls of various muscle men and eight by tens of twenty along with notes on the pictures of how she had done it with them.

"Okay, Ship. You blew that one. Take me to number two."

Nanette would not have been interested in him. He was reasonably fit, but not a body builder. She went in for bodies.

Craig said to himself, "So much for the Ship making choices. Actually garbage in and garbage out. I wasn't specific enough. I guess I might as well try number three."

Ship sent him to Janeil O'Leary. He found himself in a dormitory room with two beautiful girls studying their textbooks at separate study desks wearing skimpy baby doll pajamas that left little to the imagination. Both girls looked very attractive. Both had excellent bodies, as he could see through their sheer pajamas. He didn't know how else to find out which one was which so he said, "Janeil?"

Both girls started and turned toward him... or toward his voice. Janeil said, "Who's there?"

The other girl said, "Janeil, you know there are not supposed to boys in the dorm this time of night."

Janeil got up and came toward Craig. Craig was so mesmerized by her good looks and her vivacious body that he forgot the consequences of not getting out of her way. Instead he held out his arms and she walked right into his body where he put his arms around her in a loving sort of hug. "Mistake."

Janeil shoved herself backwards to get away from him falling on her back side and then scrambling backwards away from him. The other girl said, "What's the matter. Are you all right? Janeil. I said, are you all right? What's wrong with you? What happened?"

"Uh. I don't know. I felt like I ran into a man and he put his arms around me. I didn't, I don't see anyone and the door is still closed. I did feel him."

"Bull Shit, Janeil. Excuse my French. You've been studying too hard and needing a man. You're getting at that horny age and now you're feeling men in your head. I'm right here and there is no man here. I heard a voice calling your name and you go crazy. Don't you think you had better start dating?"

Janeil had picked herself up and was now standing looking at the door. She had not made it near the door. There was no where for anyone to hide, but she was almost afraid. No, she was afraid to go there again. "Bobby, you go to the door and see who's there if you think I'm that horny."

Bobby, the other girl, said, "Okay, Janeil. But if I don't find anything, will you admit you're just too horny?" Bobby got up and started moving with one easy motion. Craig stepped to the foot of Bobby's bed away from the path to the door. She went to the door; opened it; looked both ways up and down the hall; closed the door; and returned to her study desk and sat down. "Satisfied."

Janeil said, "I guess you're right, but I'm not horny. I'm almost a virgin. I don't have time for men in my life right now. This course in astrophysics is murderous. The math is esoteric. Maybe it was a muscle spasm from sitting here too long. Let's get to bed. I'm going to the bathroom. She left the door open behind her and Craig left to explore the hall while she was out. Bobby joined her in the bathroom and they came back together. Craig found a sitting room/television room in the other direction. When they returned they closed and locked the door and then turned out the lights in their room. Craig waited in the television room. There were a couple of girls there, but Craig did not find them interesting. He watched the news for a half hour and then blinked into the dorm room. Both girls were asleep. Craig was very physically attracted to Janeil and found her name intriguing. He knelt beside her bed. At least he presumed it was her since it was on the same side of the room as her study desk. It was warm and she slept without covers. It was dark in the room and he felt for her in the dark. She was sleeping on her back. His eyes were getting more adjusted to the dark and he could recognize her face in the moon light coming in the window. They were on about the third floor. He wasn't even sure what university this was. He lifted his hand and sat on the bed looking down on her. He bent over and kissed her on her lips. She moaned in her sleep and returned his kiss then rolled toward him. He rested his right hand on the small of her back.

He moved his hand up into the air and did not even breathe when she suddenly froze, apparently awake. She raised her hand off of his thigh and instead felt of his leg down to the knee and then down his calf toward his ankle which he had tucked up on the bed. He could see her eyes trying to see him. He knew she only saw the closet behind him.

Craig was sitting as still as he could still attempting to hold his breath.

She reached up and turned on the light on her study desk at the head of her bed. She looked around the room. Bobby stirred because of the light. Janeil turned off the light and then rolled over to face the wall.

She whispered, "Am I dreaming or is someone really there?"

Craig whispered back, "Would you do down to the TV room with me so we can talk?"

She said, "I'm not dreaming."

"Let's quietly go down to the TV room and discuss it. If we stay here we might do something we're both sorry for." He moved away and stood up. He held her hand as she got up and let herself be led by the hand down to the TV room."

"What the heck, I must be dreaming, I am holding someone's hand, but don't see a thing.

She let herself be led down the hall to the now vacant television room feeling like she was sleep walking. As he seated her on a sofa and then sat beside her with his arm around her neck, she said, "I must be totally crazy."

Craig said, "No. I am a college student and have control of some of the most amazing breakthroughs in history. I teleported here like in Star Trek and choose to remain invisible to keep my identity a secret for now."

She said, "Do you mean as in transported by breaking down your molecular structure, transmitted here like a television beam and then reassembled to less than visible."

"I guess. I don't understand it all. I'll have to check into it."

Janeil said, "You're for real." Her hand was on his thigh. "I'd like to see what you look like."

Craig said, "I want to talk some serious issues. Will you answer some questions?"

She nodded sheepishly and he asked her about her ideas on space travel. She ran her hands all over his body feeling every part of him like she was trying to memorize a shape without being able to see it. He was having a hard time concentrating on the questions. She was all for it until he said, "University of Oklahoma."

Janeil said, "Why would you be working with a back woods school like that. You're not an Okie are you?"

Craig said, "Yes, I am."

Janeil said, "I would really like to have worked with you, but there is no way I'm doing it with an Okie or going to the University of Oklahoma." As she reached up her abdominal muscles rippled and he could see just how small and muscular her waist was. Just as she had been turned off by him being an Okie, he had been turned off by her reaction.

"What's the matter with the University of Oklahoma?"

"This is Stanford. This is a real university. This isn't a dream. This is a nightmare." She left him and walked back to her room.

Craig zapped back to the ship. "Ship. That was a disaster. What were you doing, just trying to teach me that programming is an exact science and you are nothing but an overgrown computer?"

"No. I thought. Yes, I can think. I thought that if you talked with Nanette, the body builder, that she would go for you. What other man could take her to space. She is an excellent physical specimen and would make an excellent settler of new planets.

Janeil, well, I don't understand about her reaction to someone from Oklahoma or the derogatory term she called you. Okie?"

"Well, Ship, you can learn too. Makes me kind of disappointed in you and somewhat mistrusting. Okie is a term for the Oklahoma people that came to California during the nineteen thirties during the dust bowl and The Great Depression. Although most Californians probably have Okie blood, some California people have traditionally looked down on Okies as poor uneducated farmers."

11 BEACHES

He had been working long hours for a month. He needed a break. He asked the ship to select some girls for him to visit that he might find compatible and would work well on the ship in his quest. This time he asked the ship to ignore his specifications and select girls based upon his life history of girls that he had been attracted to.

Due to the hour, he went east first. It was nine in the evening. Estera Shea was studying in the library. The ship had given him the details. IQ one thirty. Body fat seven percent. Five foot five. One hundred ten pounds. Child bearing excellent. Excellent genetics. College Major, Botany. Skidmore College, Saratoga Springs, New York. Father is U.S. Representative for New York State.

He appeared, invisible across the table from her. She was very attractive. Her dark blond hair was straight, but with the last five inches swept into an inward facing curl toward her face. She had sharp features. Very long eyelashes and large sultry lips. He cleared his throat. She looked up, but only for a moment since no one was in sight. Her eyes were large and very dark blue. The library was well lit. Her face was pale, but in New York after a long winter, you would have to expect that.

He zapped back to the ship and wrote a note to her and then

zapped back and slipped the note across the table where she could see it if she looked up from her book. He then tapped the table with his fingernail. She looked up, saw the note, and then read it. She looked all around and then finished the note.

The note said, "Hello Estera Shea. I would like to introduce myself. I have three doctorate degrees and I recently had my twentieth birthday. The reason that I have doctorate degrees at my age is because I have gained a source of tremendous knowledge. I have many powers through technology unknown in our time.

I am currently working on a new serum that will eliminate disease caused by virus including AIDS and some cancers. I have provided some key changes to a formula that will replace metal as we know it. I am on a mission to move humanity into space to escape an asteroid shower that will destroy most life on Earth. I am sitting across the table from you, but I am using technology to keep me invisible and thereby not identifiable for now. If you would be interested in talking in person, then say, I love you."

Estera said, "Okay. Who are you and where are you hiding? Oh, I love you."

Craig spoke back, "Couldn't you pretend to have a little emotion when you say I love you."

"What? Who's playing jokes?" She looked under the table and said, "Where are the hidden speakers?"

Craig reached over the table and took her hand which she jerked away. Craig said, "Relax. Did you read the complete note?"

Estera hesitated and said, "Yes. You are invisible?"

"Yes. Are you naked?"

"No, I currently have on blue jeans, a knit shirt, and a wind breaker."

Estera said, "Put your hand out here again." She put her hand in his. "This is really strange. Let's go for a walk." They left the library. She left her books with another girl from her dormitory to take back for her. She led him out to a Mustang convertible and motioned for him to get in. He did. She said, "I think I should drive."

Skidmore was on the north side of town and she drove them through downtown. She said she wanted to know more about what was he was doing, but told him to not say anything. She apparently believed him because of his invisibility. He looked at the old quaint buildings. The store fronts were primarily the old wooden beamed building from years past. She drove them down to the large park on the south side of town and parked the car. They walked down the walk way between the tall trees alongside the park.

Craig said, "Your name is very intriguing, Estera. I like it."

"My daddy would have fits if he knew I was out here in the park after dark with a boy."

"No one will know."

They were walking hand in hand. Estera looked at where he should be and said, "You are right about that. I've had a very sheltered life because of my father being a Senator. That's why I came out here. I suspect at least one of the students is a spy hired to watch out after me. Thank goodness, I talked Daddy into buying me that car. We were followed you know?"

"No, I didn't know. We had better not talk here even then. We could be overheard. There are parabolic microphones you know."

"Oh. I know a place. Don't say anything, just stick close." She took them to a private hot bath at the famous Saratoga Springs Park. He followed her as she went in, showed a card and was given a key. It was a plain, very old marble room from a more glorious day. The room had its own hot tub.

Estera said, "We can talk in here. The family has always had a pass to this place. I've never been in here with a boy before, the clerks know my family. In fact, I haven't been able to see many boys anywhere. That's why I am going to Skidmore. They specialize in sheltered girls. Get your clothes off." She undid her jacket and hung it on a coat hook.

Craig said, "I wasn't propositioning you."

Estera said, "And I wasn't propositioning you either. If you try anything, there will be security here immediately. It's just that I like spending some time in the hot tub and when I turn on the bubbles it will drown out our voices, if we sit close. Now don't talk any more. Someone could here your voice outside the door." She felt for and took off his jacket. When it appeared in her hand after coming free she said, "My. Now that is amazing."

She turned it over in her hands inspecting it and then hung it on a coat hook. She then groped for his shirt and after finding no buttons, pulled it off over his head. She inspected it. She undid his jeans and slipped them down to his ankles, then removed his shoes and socks and pulled off his jeans. Then she reached for his under shorts. He tried to hold on, but she pulled his hand free. He didn't fight too hard and she didn't touch him except as necessary.

She said, "Your turn." and stood in front of him.

He hesitated and then said, "Are you sure."

Estera said, "Shhh. It wouldn't do to have anyone hear a male voice in here. I've never been undressed by a boy before. Probably because I haven't been alone with many. Now get busy or I'll have to go in with my clothes on."

Craig undid her blouse. He felt like she might be another virgin and he didn't want to be the first, especially not invisible when she didn't know him or he, her. He pulled it off over her shoulders and hung it on a hanger. She had a very tiny waist. Her skin was tight over tight muscles.

She had slipped off her shoes. He undid her skirt and let it fall. Her bra fastened in back, but when he went around behind her she spun toward him and said, "No. That's cheating."

He had to put his arms around her and struggle to get her bra off. As he pulled it free, her perfectly formed breasts came free and stood out on their own. He then pulled down her panties and she stepped out of them. She was very slender. Her waist was about nineteen inches and her legs very slim. Her buttocks, pert? She stepped into the hot tub and motioned for him to follow her. She turned on the bubbles and he followed her into the spa. It was a deep large spa with nearly straight seats around the side. It had something like foot stools in the center.

Estera said, "Sit in the middle here and no one will hear us."

He sat down in the roiling water and she sat on him facing him with one slender leg on each side of his and her breasts on his upper chest, her mouth close to his ear and his mouth next to her ear. She said, "Now we can talk. I can't see you, but I can feel that you like women. I hope you're a gentleman. Remember, don't try anything." She wrapped her legs around him and her arms around his neck. He wrapped his arms around her slender waist.

Estera said, "Now we can talk ear to ear. You feel human, even your..mmm Are you?"

Craig replied, "Yes, I was telling you the truth."

Estera said, "How do you know that there is an asteroid storm headed for Earth?"

Craig said, "I can't explain, but it was known centuries ago."

"Did you get your science from the past?"

"Yes. Good guess. People were far more advanced in the past then we are now. Humankind is only now recovering."

Estera said, "And you are trying to push science into new areas to speed the recovery?"

"Is that a good guess, or do you somehow know more than you should?"

"I have always wondered what made a few people in history burst out inventing things no one had thought of. It was them, not the organizations. Why didn't the Edison Company go on to invent television, and radar, and computers. When Edison slowed down the company slowed. Why did the space program lose its momentum when Werner Von Braun retired? Are you the next in line? Were they your predecessors?"

"Yes, they were, and yes I am next in the line. But, we are out of time. We have to get into space and soon."

"I am not a virgin. A boy had me in the boat house at our lake home. We were almost fully dressed and it wasn't much fun. "Why did you come to me? Are you just horny or is there some other reason that you came to me?

Craig said, "I need help. There is almost no way to get mankind advanced enough for space travel in only ten years. I am looking for a girl that can help me advance science. How do you feel about space travel?"

Estera said, "I'm not sure. If what you say is true, then it is critical to get into space quickly."

"How would you like to go into space yourself?"

"No. I don't think I can go into space with you, but I will help you. My father is a powerful Congressman. I can help you more as his daughter than your mate. If he knew we were here like this or if we lived together he might go against you, but as long as he doesn't know, I can be of a big help to you.

Estera said, "I will help you. My father is very powerful in Congress. I can only help you as long as my father thinks of me as his little girl. When you need something, just leave me a note or come to my room and tell me and I will try to get my father to help. You want financing of research, you've got it. You need a grant, you've got it. You want sex with me, and I'm afraid Daddy would find out and your mission to advance science will fail. Some day when you are famous, I will come see you in private. Okay? Can you get out of here by yourself?

Craig said, "Yes, but you are beautiful."

"I can help more if we stay apart. I don't have to see you. I know I will know who you are and what you look like someday. I'm leaving alone. I will talk to Daddy about the importance of funding your research. What do I tell him to fund?"

"This will give away my identity, but I guess I'm safe with you. I go to the University of Oklahoma and my research grants will come from there. Ask him to fund the grants requested by a twenty year old Ph.D. there."

"I would ask you to dress me, but after this much time, my body guard is probably in the hall now and might hear you. I believe you. Just stay here until I'm gone." She got out. Her small lithe body was very seductive and Craig didn't want her to go, but he understood her reasoning. Having legitimate money coming in would provide a cover for his possessions that the ship provided, like the Dodge Viper.

She pulled away and dressed in sort of a reverse strip tease using her slender lithe body to enhance her every move until she had dried, dressed, and left the room. Craig sat there wondering if her logic was correct and why he let her go. He then went back to the ship.

He did not visit the other girl the ship recommended out in California. He had Estera on his mind. After sleeping on the ship with a sleep learning program on Chemistry, he went to the Chemistry department head at the University of Oklahoma. Professor Gimble had already made a nuisance of himself inquiring after Craig so he needed no introduction on what he wanted to do and why. The Chemistry department head put him with another professor and two graduate assistance to help him use the equipment and chemicals in the laboratory. Craig discovered that the lab did not have the electronic equipment that he needed to develop the new chemicals he needed. The equipment had not been invented yet. The Chemistry department made some amazing advancements with what they had. Craig went back to the ship, but the ship said it couldn't provide the equipment because there was no way that Craig could just appear with new technology equipment not yet invented.

"I suggest that you take the day off and visit Sandy Scoffed. Her father can help you in the electronics department, but you would never convince him without her help. I cannot make the equipment. There is a need for you to go to her right now."

Craig took the ship's advice and zapped to California. Sandy Scoffield. IQ one twenty-three, but intuitive, and possibly much more intelligent than testing would indicate. Body fat ten percent, but arranged the way you like. Child bearing excellent. Excellent genetics. College Major, Zoology at Southern California University. Has known favorite relatives in Oklahoma so is not against Okies. Father works for Northrop Space Systems. It was ten in the morning when the ship dropped him on the beach. The ship recommended a non-invisible visit because his walking in the sand would show his presence, so he complied by ordering same. It was a deserted area of beach that could only be reached by boat. There were shear cliffs on three sides and the ocean on one side, but there was no boat visible. She was lying on the beach stark naked in the sun. He appeared fifteen feet away at the edge of the water. She was stretched out spread eagled in the sun. Her waist was also very tiny also and her legs as slender and lithe as Estera's, but her breasts were much bigger. She had very little in the way of tan lines. From what he could see of her, her swim suit must be no more than three patches of cloth tied together with strings. The ship had provided him with a skimpy Speedo swimsuit like a competitive swimmer.

Craig walked up to her, but she did not wake. The noise of the surf coming in was loud echoing off the cliffs. She did not hear him as he cleared his throat. He laid down beside her within a few inches and put his hand on her stomach over her belly button. She did not stir. She was covered only in sun tan oil and the sun glinted off her golden body and her pale blond hair. He moved his hand up her stomach and then ran his fingers between her breasts. He could see her breathing, but she still didn't stir. He traced a finger in the oil in circles around her breast moving toward the nipple. The nipple started getting harder, but Sandy still slept in the warm sun. Craig found himself getting very aroused and wanted to pull off his brief swimsuit and climb onto her, but instead put his hand on the blanket on the opposite side of her with his forearm against the opposite breast so his hand could support his weight and kissed her full on her slightly thin lips. She kissed back still without waking. His chest was touching her breasts. His legs were against her bare legs. He couldn't do it with her asleep. He moved back off her and then cupped her full opposite breast and gently rocked her. He said, "Sandy, wake up." Then when she still didn't wake he put one hand on her pelvic bone and one arm and pulled her toward him. She woke with a start.

"Let go of me. Who are you? What are you doing to me?"

Craig raised his hands and moved back a few inches.

Craig said, "I'm not here to do anything to you. How did you get here?"

Sandy said, "My boat's on the beach. How did you get here, swim?"

Craig said, "There is no boat there now."

Sandy said, "Let me up."

She sat up and looked for a moment and then ran to the water looking for her boat. She had apparently forgotten that she had no clothing. She looked very sexy. Her legs were slim and not overly muscular, but Craig could see her muscles as she ran. The hips were not too wide, but not narrow. Her buttocks were nicely formed. Her hair blew freely in the wind from the water. She splashed into the water still looking for her boat and looking like a goddess. Craig suddenly realized that he had been so concerned with her that he had not realized that when he had first arrived he was fifteen to twenty feet from her and five feet from the water and now the water was only ten feet away. The tide had come in ten feet.

She was standing in the water fighting the waves that crashed into her splashing up to her shoulders. She came walking back slowly. Craig was still lying on her blanket watching her as she came back toward him with the waves crashing around her. The water was now only a few feet from the blanket. She looked like a goddess. She looked like an apparition. A mythical mermaid coming in from the sea. She was crying.

When she got to the blanket she fell to her knees looking like she had lost a puppy. Sandy said, "How did you get here?"

Craig said, "I swam?"

Sandy said, "Where's your boat?"

"Didn't have one."

"You had to have a boat. These cliffs go for miles in both directions. The cliff is too sheer to climb."

"No. I didn't have a boat."

"Then we're dead."

Craig said, "Why would you say that? I told you I'm not here to do you any harm."

"Because the tide is coming in. At high tide the water comes all the way against the cliff wall and we would be dashed to death. Even if we survived, no one would ever find us. I've been coming here twice a week since I found this spot and have never seen another boat around this area. Maybe you can swim out, but I'm not that good a swimmer. The way the tide funnels in here, you might not be able to swim out either. If you can, you had better start swimming now."

She had apparently forgotten she was naked. Craig said, "Sandy, relax. I won't let anything happen to you. Let's walk back toward the cliffs and stay dry for awhile at least." Sandy stood up in all of her naked glory completely unconscious of her golden naked beauty. Craig gathered up her towel, baby oil, and book. He noted that the book she was reading was "Lucifer's Hammer". Craig had read that book years ago. How appropriate, it was an excellent book about the results of pieces of a comet striking the Earth. What was coming was a hundred times worse. If she had read much of the book, she would recognize the danger of an asteroid storm being only ten years away. Craig said, "How far have you gotten in your book?" holding it up for her to see.

Sandy was taken aback by his comment, "I just finished it before I went to sleep. Don't try to appease me. You don't realize that we only have another hour or so to live." As they walked along the almost flat sand, the waves covered the spot where her blanket had been. I had a small Sunfish sailboat that I have been sailing along the coast here for nearly a year. I found this place at low tide. There are a lot of rocks out there that keep the bigger boats away from this area. Because of the way the tides work, this area gets scoured once a day leaving the beach perfectly clean each day. If you think the tide comes in fast, you should see it go out. Because no one comes here, I could sail my little Sunfish in here. There are almost no waves at low tide because of the other cliffs. It has been my private place to sun in total privacy. You are the first person that's ever seen me here."

By now they were up against the cliffs as far as they could get from the advancing water. Craig said, "Where are your clothes?"

"They were in the boat. Did you see a boat when you came in?"

"No."

"You had better get out of here while you can. It's your only escape. I am telling you I know the water comes crashing in here at high tide. There will be no escape then."

"And leave a goddess like you? Never."

"Thank you for the complement, but this is not the time. Get out of here while you can." The water was getting close and Craig could see the waves growing angry as the tide came in. This really was a dangerous place to be at high tide. Just as the low tide water was calm because of the surrounding cliffs, the high tide water was apparently funneled in here violently. The water was almost to them.

Craig said, "It's too late to swim out. Before we die, will you close your eyes thinking of a better place and give me the best kiss and hug you can so I can die in peace."

She did. Craig dropped her blanket as she almost savagely kissed him. He put his arms around her waist and fought to keep from being pushed down backwards. Craig checked to make sure her eyes were closed, and then zapped them out of there. The sound of the waves was still present, but when he opened his eyes briefly they were on a tropical beach with coconut trees and palms. Instead of a cold breeze coming in on the crushing tide against the cliffs they were bathed in hot sunlight on the beach. In a few moments a warm gentle wave made it far enough up the beach to gently wash over their feet. Craig was into the kiss at first hugging her now chilled wet naked body, then he had to tell the ship by thought that he wanted to get them away to a deserted safe island in the South Pacific. Since he knew what happened, he briefly opened his eyes to see the scene and then got back into the kissing and hugging. The sun was warm against her back and on his hands. The kissing got more intense for several minutes. Craig was aroused, but kept waiting for her to realize the new location and therefore was partially faking the passion. She was not faking. She was kissing him fervently because she thought it was the last in her life. Eventually, she opened her eyes.

"What? Where are we?" Sandy let go of his head and back where her hands had been during the kiss and backed away. He let go of her waist and let her back up. She looked around at the gentle waves lapping at the beach and the incredible blue of the water in a quiet barrier reef surrounded lagoon and at the gently slope up the beach at the palm and coconut trees. "How did we get here?" Looking directly at Craig, "What is happening? Did you do this? What did you do to me? I thought we were trapped on my private beach."

Craig waited for her silence and then answered, "Yes. We were on your private beach. I was sent to rescue you." Sandy was still not conscious of her nakedness, or it didn't bother her to be naked. Maybe she was a nudist.

"How? Who sent you?"

"I didn't mean to say someone sent me. Maybe it was fate for us to meet. I cannot explain how. It is like being teleported like in the Star Trek series and movies. I teleported onto your beach and then when I discovered the trouble you were in I teleported both of us out."

"Teleportation is impossible. Besides, you have no equipment." She was looking down at his brief swim suit. Then she saw his arousal, "I mean, uh, no teleportation equipment."

Craig blushed even though he was not naked. "My teleportation equipment is remote. I have brain wave contact with it."

"Where are we?"

Craig said, "I'm not exactly sure. Supposedly some safe and deserted South Pacific island."

"Why here? I'm sorry. You saved my life. If I have this straight, I went to my private secluded spot to lay in the sun." She suddenly realized her nakedness. "I don't usually run around without clothes, but I never saw anyone near that little secluded beach before." Craig could tell she thought about trying to cover up, but there was no point since she had nothing to cover herself. "Anyway, I finished reading my book and just closed my eyes for a few moments. I guess I overslept and my boat must have washed out to sea as the tide came in. If you had not arrived when you did, I would have drowned. I owe you my life, but I can't believe teleportation."

"There are a lot of things about me you wouldn't believe."

Sandy said, "We had better get out of the sun. It's hot." They ran to the welcome shade of the trees." It was seventy yards to the trees. The pearly white sand was hot underfoot. The temperature was high as was the humidity. They arrived laughing and sweaty. She put her arms around his neck and leaned against him as he leaned against a tree trunk. "You sure picked a beautiful island. Are we going to play "Blue Lagoon"? She suddenly pulled his swim suit down and said, "No fair for me to be naked and you to have clothing." He stepped out of his swim trunks. She grabbed him and then ran further away from the water.

He caught her in some grass next to a small waterfall spilling into a pool of clear blue water. She fell to the ground with him in play. They clung to each other and then she turned her back to him. He had one arm under her waist and one arm over. They were both slick with her sun tan oil and the sweat from running in the heat and humidity. He snuggled against her backside and put the trapped hand under her waist on her abdomen and his free hand on her breast which responded with nipple erect even though she seemed to be ignoring him. She said, "Look."

He looked over her by stretching his neck. They were in a grove of trees laying in lush green grass by a sparkling pool of water at the bottom of a thirty foot waterfall. The waterfall was not vertical and the water was not swift so it didn't make much noise. Craig slid his arm out from under her so he could prop his head on his hand supported by an elbow not he ground as he too was mesmerized by the beauty of the place. As their breathing slowed they both recognized the total silence of the place. The only sound was the water running down the waterfall into the pool at the bottom and the gentle stream flowing out of the pool toward the ocean. They could not hear the surf. They lay that way for a long time. Sandy then reached back for his arm and laid her head on his arm. He lay beside her. He fell asleep.

He woke alone. Sure he was very tired after the last week, but she was a goddess on a deserted island in the South Pacific. It was probably because there was no pressure on him to perform sexually. There was no fear of discovery here. They were both safe and there was no hurry. He would not force himself on her. He had been physically and mentally tired. He called out, "Sandy?"

She answered from the pool, "I'm here. The water is cool and I'm afraid I'm sunburned from falling asleep on my beach before you rescued me. You had fallen asleep and I didn't want to disturb you. This water feels cool and good."

He got up and walked down to her. His swim suit was back on the beach so he felt self conscious walking down to her. She had found a flat rock reclining off into the pool with just a mist from the water fall. She motioned for him to join her and he did. Sandy said, "What are you planning for me? Are you going to strand me here and then zap away keeping me your sex prisoner here?"

"No. Of course not. I just wanted a private place to talk with you."

"So talk."

Craig told most of the story leaving out the story of the ship and the other girls. He told some of the things that he had done to improve the world and what his overall mission was. She listened with rapt attention.

"I want to go into space with you. Will you take me as your wife?"

Craig was afraid that she was so agreeable because of the situation and a feeling of being trapped. Any man would be attracted by her beauty. The setting was perfect. No amount of talking lying in the cool mist of the waterfall next to this goddess would discourage his arousal. Craig said, "I know your opinions now and you know my story. Can you introduce me to your father so I can get his help to invent the electrical equipment that I need to develop the new chemicals required for my anti-virus serum?"

"Absolutely. But first I want you to "Zap" away to prove you can do it." He did and came right back after a few seconds.

"Where would you like to zap to now that we have had the opportunity to talk in private?"

"Let's just stay here for awhile. Can you transport us some food?"

"What would you like?"

"How about some prime rib with a baked potato with only butter and salt and some Lancer wine?"

"Coming right up" The meal appeared on a low table in the grass along with some cushions to sit on.

Sandy said, "That's amazing. You really can teleport people and things. I wasn't just drugged and taken here. Either that or I died on that beach and gone to heaven.

They sat on opposite sides of the low table Japanese style and ate the meal in silence. She was a goddess sitting across the table from him with only her bond hair hanging down over her bare breasts. She was sweating disproportionate to the heat because of the rich food, the wine, and her sunburn that was now turning red.

Craig said, "Let's do something about that sunburn." She got up stretched her lithesome body and went back to the rock by the water. The sun was getting down around four in the afternoon and the cool ocean breezes were wafting over the island through the trees. Ship told him about a natural remedy for sunburn. He took some leaves and squeezed the juice out of them. She stretched her arms over her head accentuating her tiny waist and big breasts.

Sandy said, "I could spend my life here. I love the sun and the privacy."

"How about some natural aloe sunburn lotion, right out of the jungle?"

Sandy said, "I'm ready and I need it." She did not move. When Craig placed the cool liquid on her stomach she chilled and said, "Oooo, that feels good." It was not greasy, but slick. It was thicker than sun tan oil and clung to her body in clumps until Craig smoothed it out. She stayed stretched out. He spread it over her top first loving every inch and getting harder then he went down her top and outside of her legs down to her toes and then up the insides of her legs. When he reached the apex she said, "Take me. Take me now. "And reached out for him.

Craig complied. They drifted off to sleep intertwined into each others arms.

It was cool and nearly dark when she woke waking Craig in the process. There was only the moon to see by. She was raised up on one hand looking at him. He could only see darkness, where her face was but her light blond hair glowed in the moonlight backlighting it. He could see the moon glinting off the slickness from the aloe still on her side. The shadows highlighted her breasts and narrow waist. She said, "I don't want to ever leave this place. I could live here with you forever."

Craig broke the magic, "I have a mission. I have to save humankind. Remember?"

"Will other planets have islands like this that we can go to?"

"I have no idea. I would hope so. From all I know, we should be able to find such a place out there." They both looked up at the incredibly clear stars. There was no pollution and no electric lighting to interfere with their view of the stars.

Sandy resignedly said, "Okay. We can come back here until we get into space can't we?"

Craig said, "This might be a one time experience that we could not repeat no matter how we tried. It could be disappointing the second time."

"You're right of course. Can you support a wife? Never mind, anyone that can manufacture a meal like that from packed matter and teleport can do anything. You were serious about having that mission. Okay, what can I do to help you? I'll go with you even if not as your wife you know."

"I hope you will understand that I don't know who will be my wife. I hope you don't think I took advantage of you."

"Craig, I think maybe it was the other way. I took advantage of you. There has never been a more romantic setting and everything after the beach has made this the best day of my life. I really want to go into space and explore planets. I wasn't saying I would be your wife out of love, only wanting to go to space. I think that maybe at this moment I could love you as a husband though. Right now, I would live here on this island, just the two of us forever. Is that love, or lust?"

12 ELECTRONICS

It was mid morning back in California. He could not teleport her to her apartment because he discovered that her family was there. Her friends had known she had a private place somewhere that she went on her little boat. When she had not returned in the afternoon they had called for a search and rescue and alerted her family. Craig had the ship manufacture clothing similar to what she had and then teleported her back to the campus into an empty rest room. When she walked in to her apartment, her father wanted to know where she had been. Everyone was extremely upset at her.

She kept her silence and finally talked her father into taking her in the car to a parking lot to talk. She told him the story of her rescue, not the part about sex. She told him about Craig and what his mission was and what he needed. He was visibly upset and thought she was lying. Craig appeared in the back seat and said, "Sir. Your daughter is telling the truth."

Mr. Scoffed said, "And how long have you been hiding in the back seat?"

Craig did not say anything, but teleported them to Sandy's private beach which was now nearing low tide. Mr. Scoffed was speechless. They had been sitting in his car and the next moment they were standing on an isolated beach surrounded by cliffs. They all staggered just a bit, but Mr. Scoffed fell down. He was obviously just dazed by the sudden change. Craig said, "Sir, she was telling the truth. I rescued her off this beach at high tide, and I do need your help."

"How did we get here? What kind of a trick is this?"

"Sir, this is not a trick. I teleported us here to prove that Sandy was not lying and to show you that my mission is real. I can and do produce wonders you would not understand, but it would not do any good unless I can advance Earth science to produce it on its own. I can not mass produce the things I need in the quantities needed. Right now I need a new chemical that I can produce a small amount of. That chemical will enable the manufacture of a new serum that will prevent harmful virus. I cannot produce enough for manufacture of the amount of serum to eradicate human virus. To manufacture it I need to produce a new chemical composition. To produce that chemical I need electronic equipment that is not yet available. I can produce one or ten of these pieces of equipment, but not enough for mass manufacture of the serum. The difficult thing is a new form of transistor not yet manufactured. If you agree to help, I can supply the methods to manufacture this new transistor and the equipment I need. Will you help?"

"Can I see something about this?"

"Certainly. Will you mind if we transport to your office at Northrop so I will have room to spread out the plans?"

"Of course not." An instant later they were in his office and Craig had the drawings and design for making the new transistor and the equipment he needed. Mr. Scoffed was not as shocked by the change in scenery this time. He opened the drawings and got more and more excited.

Finally Mr. Scoffed said, "These are marvelous. We have been trying for something like this for our space program here at Northrop, but the secret eluded us. How did you get these designs?"

"I can't answer that, but they aren't stolen. Actually they are computer generated out of a special computer that only I have access to."

Mr. Scoffed said, "It will take several weeks, but yes, I know I can sell this to the brass and we will manufacture what you need. We will need a contract to exchange equipment for design. We will give you the equipment in direct exchange for us getting to use the design and sell it to other customers. Does that sound okay?"

"Yes, but you must not overprice it. There is no R&D to recover here. I provided the breakthrough. This will advance computer speed by a factor of one thousand."

"Are you going to negotiate the contract with my company? I'll verify to the value of your designs here."

Craig produced a paper and said, "No. Here is a power of attorney so you can contract for me. Okay?"

"How do you know you can trust me?"

"Because I know your daughter. She trusts you, so I trust you."

"Why can't you be here?"

"I have a lot of other work to do and not enough time to do it."

Sandy said, "When will I see you again?"

"I'm not sure. I have so much to do." He zapped them back to the car and himself back to the ship to think.

13 REFLECTIONS

Craig decided that he was moving too fast on finding a mate and that he was not working hard enough on the science that would be required to get mankind into space. You don't find a mate by going to bed with them or spying on them. You must learn them in a more normal situation to see if you are compatible. Craig planned to take his more advanced ship into space with his mate to explore the galaxy for inhabitable planets while the ships of Earth were being built. That meant being alone with a girl for weeks? Months? Years? What if he found no inhabitable planets or he was not able to get man into space. Adam and Eve? They had better be compatible. He would have to spend time with them, each of them to make sure that they were not just suited for going into space, but to make sure they were compatible with him. Did they like the same books? Did they like the same movies? Could they talk about the future with the same likes and dislikes? He determined that he would start a more conventional relationship and forget this invisible visitor stuff.

Craig decided to call a meeting with Mr. Scoffed - Nuclear Propulsion and Electronics and Professors Myrtle - Metallurgy, Davis Aerodynamics and Spacecraft Construction, Gimble - Microbiology and Medicine. He also needed to invite Representative Shea, Estera's father from New York as the chairman of the House Ways and Means Committee. It was important that he know of what was going on the urgency of the situation. However, he did not know how to get his attention and understand the seriousness of the situation.

Craig decided that he would have to talk with him personally and somehow make him a believer. The President knew about Craig, but that did not mean that he could control the Representative. He would have to contact Estera again. He checked the time, 10:15 PM. "Ship. Where is Estera and what is she doing?"

"She is at her parents' home for the weekend. She is watching television in her bedroom."

"Take me there, visible." The next moment he was there standing in front of the television. He had forgotten to give further instruction and the ship knew that she knew his identity now and that she had seen pictures of him.

Estera looked totally surprised but quickly got her composure and said, "Hello, Craig. Now I get to see you in person. You were the one I met a few months ago and you didn't forget me."

"No. That was something else. I won't forget that night."

"Then you haven't forgotten that I said we should not see each other again."

"No, but I needed to speak with you in person quickly."

"So, you can spy on me at any time to know that I was alone?"

"Uh, Yes. But, I don't watch you all the time. I just checked to see if you were alone and popped in for a talk."

"Keep your voice down. What do you want?"

"I need you to tell your father about me, everything…except that night. I need his full cooperation immediately and I want him to come to a meeting starting Monday, in Oklahoma."

"What's the rush? How can I tell my father we met? This is putting me at risk. Is it important to your mission?"

"It is critical. I just had the thought, 'if we had full international backing and everyone started producing space ships right now, how many people are going to escape? A few thousand? A million? Two hundred? See my point?"

"You mean that most of the population of Earth will still be here and will not escape. No, I … I'll go find him now. What do you want me to do?"

"Just tell him you know me, get him alone, and that I know about a calamity. Tell him I can teleport and then summon me when you want me to appear. I'll be there. Okay? And, I will call the President and have him confirm my identity and some of my power. I need his help now, ready?"

Estera nodded and immediately went to the door and downstairs to her parent's television room. Both of her parents were there watching television and Estera did not have the nerve to speak in front of both of them and have to answer their questions. Also, Craig had not said to tell her parents, only her father. "Dad? Could you come into the study and talk with me for a moment?"

"Sure, honey. What about?"

Mrs. Shea asked, "What about, Estera? Can't you ask in front of me?

"No, Mom. This strictly some questions about political policies for a report back at school. You know how you hate to discuss Dad's working buddies.

Representative Shea followed his daughter into the study and Estera closed the door behind them. He sat in his leather sofa and patted the seat next to him holding out an arm for Estera to sit under. "Okay, Estera. Ask away?"

"I lied, Dad. I have something to tell you. I met this boy in the library at Skidmore and he told me and showed me some things that will change the world in our lifetime."

"This is about politics?"

"No, Dad. Just let me tell you the story without interruptions, okay? Well, how can I say this? I had the feeling that someone was watching me as I sat in the library studying. Then, I heard a tap and found a note lying on the table opposite my chair, but there was no one near the table and I had not seen anyone near my table. I even looked under the table. The note said that he was invisible and sitting across from me. Dad…let me finish the story. I thought it was a prank so I looked for hidden speakers under the table because I hear someone say something.

Then he offered to hold my hand. I played along with the joke and held out my hand. He took it in his…but I couldn't see him. Dad…No I was not drunk or taking drugs. I'll prove it to you. Anyway, I believe him when he says he is on a mission to save the Earth from an Asteroid crash that will destroy life as we know it. Dad…don't say it. Let me finish. Do you remember hearing about that boy in Oklahoma that was awarded three simultaneous doctorate degrees?"

"Yes, Estera. I remember thinking about how that was a publicity attempt by the University of Oklahoma. Are you telling me that this invisible person is the same one and you met him as invisible?"

"Yes, Dad. I know you don't believe me. There is only one way to prove this to you. Dad, look toward your desk. Craig, now." Craig appeared on command standing about five feet from Representative Shea who stared at him like he didn't see him and then looked for the mirrors.

"No, Sir. I'm not a practical joke or an optical illusion. I would like to shake your hand to prove that I am solid and not an apparition." Representative Shea dumbfounded, held out his hand to shake hands. Craig walked up and grabbed his hand and pumped it up and down with a firm handshake. "I need your help. I know you can't believe me even though I demonstrated my invisible capability, but if you will come to a meeting with the professors at the University of Oklahoma this week starting on Monday, you will see for yourself what is happening and why your help is needed. Please keep the meeting a secret. Don't tell anyone about the asteroid part. Just explain that you are going to Oklahoma to meet this new PhD for a photo op and you can see for yourself."

"Well young man, Craig, is it. I'm not used to someone popping so much on me at once and I do have important things going on that I find it rather presumptuous of you to presume I would cancel on a whim."

"Daddy, please. This is the most important thing in all of our lives. You have to go. Don't you realize that the Earth is coming to an end? Nothing is more important than your being there."

"Estera. I don't know how you really met this young fellow or what he means to you, but I am not about to change my other meetings to go running off to Oklahoma."

"Sir, you must come. I have let things go too far without your support already. How would you feel if the President recommended it?"

"That would be different of course. Are you telling me that the President knows about this asteroid of yours and hasn't told anyone?"

"No sir. I have not told the President, but I have been working with him on the massive drug control work and the capture of Iran's leader. He will tell you that part is true and that I am for real. Okay?"

"I have a hard time getting through to the President sometimes. Do you honestly think that you can on a Saturday night? In fact, if I'm not mistaken, he is currently at a state dinner."

"Sir, would you like to see me dial the number before I get him on the line?"

"Yes. Not that I believe you."

"I'll put it on speaker phone so you can hear the entire exchange." Craig dialed the special number at the National Military Command Center that he had been given to contact the President at any time of day or night.

"NMCC, Captain Jorgensen here."

"Captain, listen very carefully. This is Craig Decker. I am calling from Representative Shea's home and I must talk to the President now. Tell him my name and he will make time right now."

"Listen, Mr. Decker. I don't know how you got this number, but the President is not available right now."

"Captain, this is a matter of national security. Tell someone that I am calling and I say it is important. He will take the call. I'll wait. Now do it." The telephone went apparently dead, but there was no dial tone or click as in a cut off. It stayed that way for three minutes while Representative Shea got more impatient and Estera held his hand to keep him from hanging up the telephone.

Then the President's voice came on, "Craig. It's your nickel. I understand that you said it was a matter of national security, so I left the Prime Minister of England and the Prime Minister of India sitting at the table to take this call privately. What can I do for you?"

"Sir, I mean, Mr. President. I need Representative Shea to come to a critical meeting tomorrow in Oklahoma. I do not want to tell you what about yet. I want Representative Shea to be in on the start of this new thing first, even before you. Could you approve that and tell the Representative that it must be critically important for me to call on you."

"Sam. Are you there?"

"Yes, Mr. President."

"Sam. I don't know what this is about and I don't know why Craig wants you to know something before I do, but if that's the way he wants it, I owe him one or two. Will you go, for me?"

"Yes, Mr. President. If you agree that this is that critical I will. Do you want me to brief you on the outcome of this meeting?"

"Only when Craig says he's ready and then I would like him to be with you. If that's all, Sam, Craig, I'd better get back to my dinner before the guests declare war on each other."

Craig said, "Thank you, Mr. President. One of the things we will discuss this week is when to bring you in on it. Sorry to have bothered you."

"No bother, Craig. I said I owed you a couple. I still owe you." Craig hung up the telephone, turned off the speaker phone, and then patiently looked at Representative Sam Shea.

Sam Shea looked thoughtful for a moment. His daughter was clinging to his arm, looking expectantly at him. Craig was obviously waiting for the inevitable answer. "Okay, but I want you to tell me what the meeting is about so I won't come in cold.

"Sir, this is going to be a brain storming session. The asteroid is coming for Earth and will hit in nine and half years. I have not told the President or the professors about this yet. The urgency about the situation is that I have a plan to evacuate some of the people of Earth before that time, but we can only evacuate a few. In addition to that, the technology of Earth is behind on the task. I am going to need your help and advice. I have introduced new computer technology that gives one ten thousand times the power of past computers. I have introduced a new metal that will make extended space travel safe. I have advanced the mathematical knowledge to make astrophysics capable of navigating through space. I have introduced medical technology that will eliminate AIDS and most cancer. I do not have the fuel developed yet. We do not have the funding for full production on any of this. If there were all of the funds of Earth and if everyone worked together to the exclusion of all else other than eating and sleeping I just realized that we can still only evacuate a few. I need you to attend this meeting and I need your help and advice on a number of issues. It is important for you to be there to hear the discussions so you will fully understand the situation and the factors involved."

"How did you learn about this asteroid and these scientific break throughs and how did you engineer the anti-drug wars and how were you responsible for the capture of the Iranian Leader, and what do you have planned for my daughter?"

"Sir. I cannot tell you all of the hows. The President can fill you in on some of the anti-drug and some stories about my involvement with Iran. Sir, I don't have any specific plans for your daughter. She told me to stay away from her, but I needed your help badly and she did offer to help me?"

"Estera? I think we need to talk. I'll attend your meeting and then Estera and I will have to have a long talk. In private if you don't mind. In the mean time, I'm going back to watch television like nothing happened here. Young fellow, I expect you to be out of my house and away from my daughter before I come back in here. I will see you next week." With that he pulled loose Estera's arm from his and walked out of the room without looking back. He closed the door as he left.

"Well. It could have been worse. I don't know whether father will trust me again or not. Not that he knows what happened, but I was sent to Skidmore to be away from boys, not bring in strange ones, especially not to the house. You are strange you know. How many college students can go invisible and can call the President out of a state dinner? How many can spy on people wherever they are without anyone knowing they are there. I would imagine that father is a little shook."

"Sorry, Estera. I'm sorry if I upset anything between your father and you. Maybe he will see you as a heroine. I'm sorry that I said I have no plans for you, but I don't. The last time you saw me, you said to never contact you in person. I broke the rules because I don't; WE don't have time to play around."

"I forgive you. Don't worry. I know how to handle Daddy. But now, get out of here. Don't come back unless it is critical again. I agree, this is critical. We should both have realized it earlier. You go; I'm going out to work on Daddy."

Craig returned to his dorm. He decided to stick to his earlier decision to get to know the girls better. He used the telephone to call Dawn at her sorority. "Hi Dawn. This is Craig Decker. I would like to see you more conventionally. Can you meet me out front and go down to one of the clubs on Campus Corner's?"

"If we're going to be conventional, I will say no. I don't go out much with anyone, and especially not when a boy calls at midnight asking me to go out. Actually, I was already in bed. How about taking me to church and lunch tomorrow?"

"Okay. I have decided that I would like to get to know you better as a person and stop spying on people."

"That's good. I'll be ready at 8:30 tomorrow morning. I go to the 9 o'clock service at St. Johns Episcopal. Okay?"

"Okay. I will be at your sorority door at 8:30 sharp." They hung up. Craig thought, "She's right. I was right. I need to learn to meet these girls more conventionally. Representative Shea and Estera were right about me not dropping in on people and spying on them. Having power corrupts. Having absolute power absolutely corrupts. I can still use the powers; I just have to be more diplomatic about using it. I will never get to know which girl, if any of them, I should take as a wife unless I do it from a conventional stand point. I have already biased them with my tricks. Jill and Shelby and maybe none of them would have paid me any attention if I were the old Craig Decker, sophomore at OU, with no money and a limited future.

It was not midnight as Dawn had said; it was really only 11:30. Craig needed to be asleep by 3 o'clock AM to take Dawn to church at 8:30. He had three and a half hours to kill. He zapped to the ship to look in on the California goddess to see if she was free. It was only 9:30 in California. "Maybe she will go out with me this evening?"

"Hello, Sandy? Craig Decker here."

"Craig! I have been sitting here at my apartment every night for months waiting to hear from you. When Dad called to say that you had invited him to a meeting I begged to go with him, but he declined. Said I had to get my own invitation. Why didn't you just teleport in on me instead of calling?"

"Sorry I haven't contacted you. I telephoned to see if you would be willing to go out on a normal date with me so we can get to know each other. It's not right for me to just teleport in."

"Of course. How soon can you get here?"

"I'm just stopping in the parking lot now. I'm on a cell phone. If you see a red Mustang convertible, that's me waving."

"I'm coming now. Wait, where are we going on this 'date'?"

"Wherever you want. I want to go somewhere you like so we can get to know each other in a more normal setting."

"How about right here?"

"Sandy. I just want to visit and have some normal fun. It would not be right to come up there."

"I guess the desert island is out too then. Okay, I'm coming, as is. I know a place we can go." Sandy came running down the metal stairs of the apartment building and ran to his car. She was wearing a skimpy bikini top and matching neon pink nylon short shorts. She had something like a scarf flapping in her hand as she ran. She paused to open the door and threw herself over the center to grab Craig around the neck and kiss him. He put his arms around her and kissed her back until she put too much of her body in his lap and jammed the car horn. He lifted her back up and toward her seat on the right. Sandy released him, "I guess the parking lot in the front seat of a convertible is not the right place either."

"No, and I crave your body too much to be alone with you. Where can we go to be in a crowd for a few hours to get to know each other mentally?"

"I know all I need to know, Craig. I'm ready now. I haven't looked at another man since I met you. I've been absolutely spellbound by studying space and asteroids and comets and space travel and thinking about how you changed my life from hum drum to excitement. What haven't you contacted me? I've been dying to see you again. You are all I've been able to think about."

"Where can we go?"

"Oh, why not the boardwalk at Redondo Beach. It's always crowded. We can walk on the beach if we need privacy. We can get a drink. Something to eat. We can go out on the fishing pier. Take your choice. Just follow this street straight west. It dead ends there. Now. Tell me why you haven't been back until now."

"Sorry, Sandy. I've been rather busy. I have thought about you, but I am also afraid of you. Afraid for you. I don't think it was right for me to take advantage of you after saving your life. I still crave your body, but we don't know each other at all. How do you know you want anything to do with me really?"

"You want to save the world. You have the power and knowledge. You are not after power and money. You just gave my dad the biggest computer breakthrough in history that would be worth millions if not billions. We work physically. What else do I need to know?"

"What kind of music do you like?"

"Oh that kind of thing. Whatever you like."

"You're missing the point. If we were to go off into space, possibly for years trapped together in a spaceship could we make it without killing each other over some petty thing? Would you really be happy? Would I?"

"Well, if you like my body, you should see my mother. She's forty-five and still turns heads. I don't have to diet; I was born with this body. My mother doesn't have to work on hers and she's had three kids. Oh, all right. I play the Viola and like classical music for reading. I really dig alternative rock. I don't like rap with all of its swear words. A lot of my friends like country, but I don't own any, but on the other hand, I don't need to because some of my friends play nothing else. I have never been into opera, but I could learn to like it. How about you? Oh, turn right here and go to the next light, then turn left and look for parking."

"Well, we agree on music, except I'm a little stronger against rap, country music and opera. I don't like any of them, and I suspect you don't either. I read the book, "Lucifer's Hammer" several years ago. It's going to be worse than that you know. Anyway, apparently we agree on books. Do you go to church?"

Sandy paused, "No. Do you? I mean I was raised going to church; it's just that I don't like any of the churches around here. They keep preaching about helping illegal immigrants and sending money overseas. I think we need to keep this country strong. I believe in God and Jesus Christ and the Bible and all. It's just that I don't like the churches recently."

"Okay. We agree again, except that there are some churches I have been going to that don't preach things I can not believe in. Illegal immigrants aren't an issue in Oklahoma. Yes, they do send money to missionaries overseas, but they don't go on and on about it and spend most of their money on local community things. A little too much concern for the homeless, maybe. Here we are. Now where? They were actually south of Redondo Beach and parked at a beach. There were plenty of people on the boardwalk which was lined with little cafes and shops. There were people scattered here and there across the expanses of beach. There was a one group of college age kids having a party with kegs of beer and barbecue grills. He could not hear their music, but a number were dancing some kind of dance that looked really strange from a distance without hearing the music they were dancing to.

"I'm hungry. There's a good Italian place right around the next corner north."

As Craig ran along with her hand in hand he thought, "We don't know each other well enough, but Sandy certainly looked like she was in total love with him. She was very happy, even bouncy, and crazy in love with him and obviously overjoyed at his return. How could he not be in love with her? It made him feel great. She was a goddess. Tanned, shapely, blond, blue eyes, the right size in all ways. She was intelligent. Any guy that felt as loved by her as he did would have to have his head examined for not returning her love. Yet, he was maybe too awed by her looks. He wasn't that bad looking. He thought of himself as good looking, but not really muscular. Oh he was afraid of no one and could handle any other one person. He had played nose guard despite his size. But he was too clinical. He was studying her versus just letting his libido go. Maybe there had been too many girls too quickly? Was power going to his head? Craig heard himself saying, "Yes, just spaghetti will do fine. Yes, we'll take a carafe of your house wine. No, I'm not over twenty-one. How about iced tea."

"Nice try, Craig. Do they let you order wine in Oklahoma?"

"No. They usually don't even ask adults except at very nice restaurants. Remember, Oklahoma hasn't always been a wet state."

"I hadn't thought about that. Did I tell you that Daddy will be staying with his sister when he comes to your meeting next week? No, I didn't. Anyway, how does it feel to be calling a meeting of distinguished scientists at your age? Never mind. I wish I could be there. Did you know that I run my own web site? I'll bet you didn't know that I finished my sophomore year in my first year here in college. I know that's nothing compared to having three PhD's at your age, but …I'm rattling aren't I?"

"Yes, but I'm enjoying it. I did want to get to know you better didn't I say?"

"Okay. I feel like I've been bottled up since we met. I started taking CLEP tests. I've found myself immersed in study. I want to catch up with you. They would only let me enroll in twenty-two hours, so I'm taking another sixteen by correspondence. Daddy thinks I'm going to fast. Do you? Anyway, I sleep, eat, go to class, study, and read. I've quit television; they don't even know what we know. All of the dramatic shows and the news are so shallow compared to an asteroid wiping out the Earth in only a few years. I told you that I have been studying it. The Yucatan peninsula is a leftover from the strike that may have killed the dinosaurs, but you knew that. Hudson Bay may have been formed by a comet or asteroid strike…I'm rattling again. I'm excited. You're exciting." She put her hand in his lap as their food arrived. When the waiter was gone she said, "You do like me don't you? Are you sure you don't want to go somewhere more private?"

Craig said, "Yes, I do like you. I like your talking. I love to hear your voice. I love to feel your body next to mine, but I just want to keep talking. I am not all that smart. I know a lot, but I had a lot of help learning. Maybe I will be able to show you someday how I learned. I agree with your dad. You are plenty smart. If you had the advantage I had you would have multiple PhD's also. Don't work so hard. You need to slow down and enjoy life. No, don't cry. I like you very very much, I don't love anyone else. I'm not trying to dump you. I'm just not sure that we are in love. Lust yes, love no. We don't know each other well enough. I have agreed with everything you have rattled about so far, just keep going unless you have a few questions for me." Craig thought, "I knew I shouldn't have done it with her. Now I feel responsible."

She had clouded up for a moment and then brightened. "Craig. How do you feel about me?"

Craig thought, "Uh Oh", but said, "I am very attracted to you physically. I have heard nothing from you that I disagree with at all. I know of no reason that we could not get along on a lonely spaceship. I know the bed part would be good, but I hardly know you. I can't honestly say that I have ever really been in love. No one has attracted me physically more than you, but maybe that was due to the circumstances of our meeting. If it had not been for that we would not have met. If we had met at a party or just walking along from opposite directions out there on the boardwalk, I would have undressed you with my thoughts, but you would not have noticed me except as an obstacle to go around. I am feeling guilty about making it with you on that desert island. That was totally unfair to you. I had just saved your life. You were vulnerable. You are not making me feel any better now about my taking advantage of you. I am feeling like I am obligated to you."

"Well, Craig. We're finished eating. I suggest we go for a moonlight walk on the beach. I promise I'll keep quiet until we get to the water. I know the owner here. She'll keep our shoes safe until we can get our feet washed off." They left their shoes and walked across the rough dry sand to reach the packed wet sand at the edge of the gentle waves washing up occasionally around their feet. They walked away from the parties though there were a few people lying on blankets higher on the beach.

"Craig, I have been thinking. I was not a virgin when I met you, but you know that. I have had a few close boyfriends that I had sex with. I have never taken drugs and I have never been drunk. You were the only one that I did not know long before having sex with. There have been only two others actually. There was never excitement between us which we came to realize before getting married or something. I went with a boy for three years in high school before we had sex, but it was a chore neither of us enjoyed much. We drifted apart before the prom. I didn't go to the prom. I had a wild summer out here after high school before college and met a boy that I really liked and he liked me. He went back east to college while I stayed here. He came home once after the first month. We went out. We had sex. He went back east and did not come home for Thanksgiving or Christmas and I didn't write him. That's not fair to him. He wrote me weekly from the time he left for college, but summer was over for me, I never replied to his letters. I had sex with him in payment for the good summer, but I didn't really miss him once I started to college. I had turned into a loner. I know I can attract any man at any time. Wherever I go men stare. Men make advances any time I slow down enough for one to catch up to me. You are right, I would not have noticed you along the boardwalk, but then I would not have noticed any other man. I might have noticed a few other pretty girls that I would see as potential competition. I always thought I could have any man at any time, but you are the first one I really really wanted and the first to not want me in return. No. That's not right. I know you want me physically, but I also understand your questioning whether it is love. I have been sitting for months waiting for you. I know you have had a lot on your mind. You alone are responsible for saving Earth. I don't have that worry on me because I could not save Earth if I tried. I would like to help you. I have been studying to make myself useful. I know I cannot take on your responsibility, but I wanted to learn whatever I could that might be of help. Even if you decide you don't want me at all, I will still want to be ready to help in any way I can. Getting as many as possible off this planet is the most important thing in this life right now."

Craig grabbed her arm stopping them. He pulled her to him, put his arms around her waist and kissed her like there would be no tomorrow she melted into him. They became as one. Time flew by, but they were not aware of it. Neither could later recall how long they held that passionate kiss, but passersby that had not been in sight earlier interrupted them. Craig said breathlessly as they broke off their kiss, "I think that must be a record long kiss. I think I had better take you home while we can still get there."

They went hand in hand. Craig could not take his eyes off her hair, her eyes, her body, oh her body. She didn't talk. They got to the car without another word. Craig felt like they floated there. He mechanically drove to her house. He was bewildered. He didn't really know her. She was more gorgeous than any girl he had imagined, even in the movies. She was smart. They had an attraction like two super magnets of opposite poles, but the very attraction put fear into his heart that he would forget who he was and what the mission was. Was this what had stopped Edison or Von Braun? A woman?

Craig walked her to her apartment and said, "I think it would be better if I did not come in. Yes, I think I am in love with you. Everything. But I'm so infatuated with you that I am also terrified. I am terrified that I will lose my very sole in your love. I'm terrified that I will forget my mission.

Others before me have lost the mission. I cannot lose the mission. I am Earth's last hope. Please try to understand. I want you *too* much. I promise you will be one of the ones going into space, but if I continue seeing you I will not have a hope of saving Earth. Actually, right now, I may not be able to even save a large number of humans. Time is running out. The ten years that I had is slipping through my fingers. Please understand. Don't wait for me. If you find someone else I will understand. Don't cry either. I promised that you will be going into space either with me or your new boyfriend if you have one. You are too much for me at this time. I have be scientist first, male later. I also have be honest, you are the only girl I have ever had sex with, but I have been looking for other girls. I cannot take anyone with me except a wife and I am the first to be allowed to do that. Right now I am confused. She has to be like you, attractive, intelligent, and adventurist."

He did not wait for her to say anything. He just left her and went to the ship.

Ship said, *"You are crying. You did a very brave thing. Yes, I have lost most of your predecessors to women. I would understand, but I am glad you understood. You were given a chance no predecessor was ever given you know. You were given the chance to marry and bring a wife here. I do not understand human emotion, but I can gauge your physical and mental condition. None of your predecessors were as physically attracted as you were to her. Your mental function all but stopped. You were probably right to break it off with her for now. Maybe in a few more months after you have made more advances."*

"Ship! Shut the heck up. That was the hardest thing I have ever done. It was like killing your young dog because you couldn't afford to feed it. No there was nothing like that. I don't know if I made a mistake. Maybe I should have brought her here. She wanted to help me. I need help. I was just afraid that I would forget to help myself. I want that girl, but I have to save the world. God! God! God!" Craig went to sleep on the sofa in the ship.

14 A NEW DAWN

It was 8:15 when Ship woke him.

"Craig. You promised to take Dawn to Church this morning. It's time to wake up and get moving."

Craig woke up feeling drained, but rested at the same time. There was a great emptiness in his heart. However, he had made the break with her. He did need help. Ship had limited his personal help on the ship to a wife. Sandy would have robbed him of thought when all he could think of was sex. He had promised Dawn that he would take her to church. "You're right, Ship. Take me down with a nice suit and tie for church. Put me in the Viper at the dorm. Now."

He was in the Viper on a deserted street only blocks from the sorority house. He needed to go to church to think. Was it all lust with Sandy? He didn't really know her. She told him all the right things for them to get along together, but he had said he needed to spend time with all of the girls he had met. Could he give Dawn a fair chance? He didn't know. Right now he was confused.

Dawn came running out to his car waving at him. Craig got out of the car to go around and open the other door for her. She did look good. He did have to admit that Dawn had a perfect body that he had seen naked. He had not made it with her and she did not apparently want to with him, which was different from the others. Maybe she was the right one. Maybe she was frigid. Maybe he should just relax. "Hello Dawn. You're looking good."

"With clothing? This is the first time you have seen me clothed in normal clothes you know."

"Yes, with clothing. You look great." He closed the door after she had gotten in. It was cold this morning in Oklahoma. Not like last night in California. Talk about jet lag. He had only slept for two hours last night.

Driving to the church Craig asked, "Were you raised in the Episcopal Church?"

"No. I thought that I was caught in a small town and went off to an Episcopal high school in Vicksburg, Mississippi." We had to go to church twice a day. I like it because the sermon is short." They were there. They went in with very little talk. Craig followed her lead in lowering a kneeler and praying with her elbows resting on the pew ahead.

"God. Why me? This is such a responsibility. Why couldn't finding a mate wait? If you could guide me, I wouldn't have to find a mate to take to the ship. I need advice. I need to find a mate. None of the girls I have met would have met me except for Ship. Is there another girl out there? Do I pick one of the ones I have met since this all started? Which one would make the right wife? How can I choose?"

Craig was lost in thought and had apparently dosed off right after the start of the sermon when Dawn elbowed him, "Craig wake up." she whispered.

Craig woke up. He had not gotten enough sleep last night, but now he was fully awake. After church as they were walking out, Dawn said, "Just like a man. Falling asleep in church. You have a good voice. Are you a singer?"

"No. I was in high school. I was the lead bass. Our first tenor, second tenor, and baritone all got college scholarships for their singing. I was not interested."

"Why not?"

"Well. I never sang popular music and I don't like opera. What else is there, music teacher?"

"Got a point there, Craig. Before you got involved in all this what were you going to do?

"I thought about being a medical doctor, but decided I would not have the money to go to medical school so I enrolled in Aeronautical Engineering, but then I did not like engineering, so I was a non major. I don't know. I just knew that I was going to graduate in something. What about you?"

"I haven't decided yet, but I want it associated with space. I don't really care what it is. This was before we met. I just wanted to work for NASA or JPL, that's Jet Propulsion Laboratory, in any way I could. I don't care whether its aeronautics, medicine, or just as a controller on the ground. I have always wanted to go into space, but I would settle for talking with them from the ground. My major is astronomy and astral navigation. I don't think they are really ready for that many female astronauts yet. In fact, until you came along an unmanned exploration vehicle seemed the best bet. They have cancelled the space shuttle."

"Where would you like to eat?"

"Let's go to the Kettle. It is still breakfast time."

"Why did you pick astronomy and astral navigation?"

"Because I would like to navigate between the stars. I never expected to get the chance, but I have spent many years imagining space travel. I hoped that maybe I could develop some new concepts in space navigation that make me a place in history. I want to get my PhD before I get serious about a man. Once I get married and start having children, I will not have time for my studies. I always thought that I would have to get a PhD and either become a professor or go to work for NASA or JPL before I could make a name to be taken seriously. Once I have a name, then I can start thinking about marriage and children. You have upset my plan. I'm attracted by you. What do you think of Earth's chances of getting seriously into space?

"We will make it. My concern is that we can only get a few people into space before the asteroid."

"Asteroid?"

"Whoops. I slipped." He parked the Viper in the parking lot behind the Kettle which was already crowded with Sunday morning church goers and left the engine running for heat. "Yes, asteroid. There is an asteroid that is going to strike the Earth in a little over nine years that will destroy most life on Earth."

"Now wait a minute. My official position may only be a sophomore because they won't let me go fast in astronomy like you did to get your degrees. Something about paying my dues. There are no tests that I can CLEP through, except for math. I have finished the math for my bachelors. I am about as smart as you are, just not as interested in hard science. I'm more into theory and far out stuff, like the eventual space travel of man. I know about our discovered universe. I know there are a number of Earth orbit crossing asteroids. In fact, I keep track of every one discovered. I dare say that my database on asteroids is as good as any on Earth. There is no way that you can know for certain about an asteroid that will strike the Earth nine years from now."

"Way. I mean that there is a way that I can know. It's for real. People far in our past predicted the exact moment."

"Wait a minute, Craig. I know you are smart or they wouldn't have awarded all those degrees. I know that some professors are working on some ideas of yours that they are all enamored about, but you cannot read some Nostradamus and know for sure that you are interpreting him right. You're smarter than that."

"Dawn. You are stubborn, aren't you? I am not reading any history that anyone else has read to know about this. In fact I may be the only one on Earth to know about this history."

"Come on, Craig. Now you're disappointing me. I was about to give up my virginity to you because I thought that maybe you were too good to pass up and now you're sounding like an immature kid. Maybe you fooled some of the professors, but you are making me mad now. I told you I know of every single asteroid discovered to date and no one can predict nine years into the future. If you have found some historical document that no one else has ever seen, I would like you to show it to me. I didn't tell you before, but one of my earlier hobbies was reading about archeology and I have taught myself to read cuneiform, hieroglyphics, and many other ancient languages. Maybe you are just mistranslating."

"Dawn, I don't want to argue. What would you say if I told you our ancestors had an ancient computer that had the knowledge stored there and they escaped into space during a previous asteroid strike?"

"Bullshit, excuse my French. Why don't you just take me home?"

"Fine." Craig put the Viper in gear and pealed out backwards then forwards as he started back toward the campus."

"What I said, immature. What are you trying to prove? Your car is faster than someone else's."

Craig slowed down simmering in frustration. This was one very brilliant girl, but she thought he was a fake. Before Ship, he would have been too dumb to ever interest her. Now, because of Ship, he knew more than all the people of Earth, and yet, she really was more intelligent. Maybe Ship would have picked her if its creators had known that women would be the equal of men in the future. Ship had not taught of him about astral navigation. In fact, there was a good possibility that Ship actually did not know much about it. The Atlanteans left it behind as they left for space. "Damn."

"Now you are going to resort to swearing."

"No, I'm sorry. I've really been pretty stupid. I need your knowledge of astronomy and particularly astral navigation. How much do people know about astral navigation?"

"Very little actually. I made that up. There is no degree that I know of in it. It is only a specialty in mathematics and astronomy. Sort of like physical psychology is a specialty in psychology. You don't really get a degree in it. My objective is to be the first professor to actually make it into a degree program. I need more graduate level mathematics, and I don't know as much as I would like to know in astronomy, but I really think that I have the best total understanding of anyone. My professors so far seem pretty backward. It seems natural to me, but I have a hard time explaining it to astronomers. Did you know that last month I addressed an international symposium on the future of space travel and actually got an award for my presentation on astral navigation?"

"Ship is that true?"

"Yes, she is being considered for a special study program at Princeton with a very large grant. She may get her doctorate in a year, but she does not know that yet."

"Ship. What do you know about astral navigation?"

"Sorry. I have a lot of theory in my data bank, but no real knowledge. I have sensors that should help me identify habitable planets from very long range. I can navigate from dead reckoning and I can find my way back to anywhere I have been before because I can keep track of every thing we might pass, but you will have to set the general course."

"You mean, I need Dawn for navigation."

"Yes. You have made a very good choice for a wife."

"Who said, I have chosen her."

"What choice do you have but to choose her?"

"I thought that Sandra would be the one I would want once the voyage starts."

"Who's going to explore ahead of the Earth fleet of ships? Someone must chart the stars and provide a course. The Atlanteans had a hundred years to build their huge ships. They went together in only a few large ships as advanced as I am."

Craig went past the sorority house and kept driving south to highway nine where he turned and headed toward Thunderbird Lake. Dawn was not terrified of him, but had a determined look on her face. She could probably take him apart in a fight. She was smaller, but very fit and knew karate.

Dawn, "There is something I have to show you. I have come to a very difficult decision. You don't know how difficult. You do not have to be afraid. I'm not going to attack you or anything like that. I am going to show you the source of my knowledge if you will let me. It will answer all of your questions and remove all doubt about my knowledge."

Dawn relaxed her death grip on the center console and the door pull a little, "And just what is this thing you are going to show me?"

"You would not believe it until you see it."

"I know karate. I can take care of myself you know."

"No, Dawn. I have had the opportunity to take advantage of you. Relax. Trust me. I have made a very painful decision and decided that I need your help to save the people of Earth. You can not help that much until I give you access to my knowledge base."

"And just where is this knowledge base?"

"Will you trust me?"

"You are right. You saved me when I was in trouble. You've seen me with no clothing; I have a hard time saying, naked. You could have jumped me in bed at any time. Okay, but why are you heading out of town?"

"Because we need privacy where no one will see where we go. Believe me; you will not believe what I am going to show you even after you see for yourself."

On a Sunday morning on highway nine in a Dodge Viper with a young experienced driver, it does not take long to go seventeen miles to the Thunderbird dam. Craig pulled into a deserted picnic area parking lot. All of the leaves were gone, but there were enough trees to shield the view of the car from any passers by. "Dawn, I'm not sure how this works, but you will really have to trust me on this. Follow me, please. And don't ask questions, just follow direction." He led them into the trees near the front of the car. "Hold my hand."

"Won't work, Craig." Ship said. "I said wife. You have to commit to take her and you must be skin to skin, not just hand in hand."

"Great. Why don't you tell her that?"

"There has been no contact with ship. She is a woman. I am not programmed for more than one person, but I calculate that if you are holding skin to skin…not clothing to clothing, it will work just fine. I can produce plenty of food and air for twenty people, but I cannot transport her as a separate person."

"Dawn, there is a minor problem. You know how I can teleport in and out of a room."

"Yes. At least you can disappear and reappear and that time at the river you did apparently come out of a shower to teleport to the river to rescue me."

"Well, I was going to teleport you to my knowledge base, but I found I can't take you through teleportation with all of our clothes on. It will only work if we are holding onto each other…without the clothing. You will also have to agree to commit to be just like you would a husband. I will make that commitment to you. You see I will be taking you to a space ship in orbit. The ship informs me that to transport you, you have to be a wife in the ships opinion which means no clothing in transit. Remember, we have held each other before without clothing. Remember, I could have caught you naked any time I wanted, and I have several times. I need your knowledge of astral navigation to save mankind for space. Will you come with me somewhere warm where I can teleport you to the ship?"

"Wow. Talk about a stumbling attempt to ask a girl to get naked with someone. Married? That only happens in a church or a court or a justice of the peace. I'm sorry. I trust you, I think. It's not that cold."

"I said committed as if married is what the ship considers married, with being naked a prerequisite."

"As long as you are only talking about a naked hug and not sex, let's just do it right here and get it over with."

She took off her coat then turned around and said, "Zipper please."

They laid their coats on the ground and then quickly stripped down in the cold. Both stretched out on their coats for him to pull her hose off and him to pull off his slacks. It was cold. He rolled toward her as she undid her bra and then quickly grabbed him for warmth, "Do it now if you can, its cold."

15 FIRST MATE

The thought flashed through Craig's mind, "Do what now?" He said out loud for Dawn to hear, "Ship, now!"

They were suddenly surrounded by the blackness of space, but warm with no wind, or if not warm, at least not cold, they were clinging onto each other in weightlessness. Ship intercepted Craig's thoughts as he saw that the stars were totally around them.

"You are in a special room I prepared for you. It is like a glass bubble with stars all around, except that at the bottom of the bubble, the stars are hologram generated. I thought this would make a good wedding chapel for the first woman to be on board that wants to be among the stars. I will gradually turn on the gravity to bring you down on the bed after you have consummated the marriage."

"Craig thought back, "Consummate? I was going to show her the ship and then let her make the decision."

"Sorry. I will not do that. She must be your wife before I will let her see me. You can teleport back if you want."

Dawn said very softly afraid to say anything, "Where is this? What has happened? Are we in space? It's not cold, it's not warm. The only thing I feel is your body next to mine, and you said no sex."

"We are on board a spaceship that has been here for fifty thousand years. You are the first woman in all of history to be here. This is my first time to be suspended in a bubble like this surrounded by stars. The ship considers you my wife now and this the wedding chapel."

"We're weightless. It's not cold. Is this a dream?"

"No, this is not a dream. We are in space and we are in weightlessness."

"How do we get out of weightlessness? Is this your source of knowledge?"

"Yes this is my source of knowledge."

"Are you going to show me around?"

"Dawn, you must believe me. Ship just telepathically told me we have two choices. Believe me, I did not know this. We can teleport back or in order to show you the ship we are on, we must be married. The ship told me we must consummate the marriage before it will let you enter and see the ship."

Dawn did not say anything, but continued to hold him quietly. The dome rotated so that the Earth and moon came into view below (?) them. She said, "Look." She motioned with her head and as Craig craned his neck around to see her view of the Earth and moon, she started working on a hickey on Craig's neck. This completed his arousal. They made love in the weightlessness of space surrounded by the stars their bodies illuminated for each other by the reflected light of the Earth and moon. It was a consummate consummation of their marriage.

They went to sleep holding each other in weightlessness and woke on the bed where Craig had been introduced to the ship, except that it was ornately feminine this time. The bedroom was a lace covered four poster like from a queen's chamber from the past. They woke intertwined together and slowly un-intertwined. The side of the bed faced the window where they could see the Earth. Dawn said, "I believe you. Let's do it again. This time she was on top of him. They fell asleep again afterward. When Craig awoke again, he amazed at how good it had been and was trying to remember Sandy that he thought he was in love with. Dawn was across the room, still naked, sitting at a mirrored dresser worrying her hair. "Good morning, Craig. I'm ready for my tour."

"We're going to have to find some clothes if you want a tour."

Dawn turned swiveled her chair toward him as she was still reaching back brushing her hair, her breasts jutting out toward him, "Why's that?"

"Because we will never get out of the bedroom at this rate."

"There's more?" she said coquettishly. "Oh, all right. Where do I find clothing? We didn't bring any with us."

"I think if you go to that free standing closet over there, you will find whatever you want."

"How do you know what I want to wear?"

"I don't, but Ship can read your mind now."

"How do you know that?"

"Well, Ship could read my mind. I did not dream up this bedroom decor, this is obviously from your mind, not mine. I like it better than when I thought up a bedroom, but it definitely has a woman's thoughts in it."

Dawn went to there. "Wow, you are one sexy lady. I never realized just how sexy. I'd be happy to just live here in this room."

Dawn turned around holding out a see through floral long sleeve tie up blouse and matching tan short shorts. "This is the only thing in the closet. Is this your idea?"

"I don't think so, but do you like it?"

"Well yes, but I would never wear this back on Earth."

"There you have it. Ship read your mind. Apparently you want to drive me crazy, but on Earth you were not interested in attracting men."

"I do like it, but I can't find a bra and panties. What are you wearing?"

Craig was considerably more self conscious about being naked as he got out of the bed and went to a more masculine chest of drawers to find some clothing. The only thing there was a single pair of silky loose jogging shorts. He put them on.

Ships voice came out of the air, *"Welcome aboard, Dawn. Craig is the captain, but, if you will excuse the expression, you are the first mate. We are ready for the tour?"*

When Craig looked toward Dawn she was dressed in her tan loose fitting short shorts and tied together at the waist translucent floral long sleeve shirt. Her waist was thin with her ribs visible below the tied up blouse. Her breasts were quite visible, but at least semi-covered. Temporarily at least, Craig was ready for the tour.

Dawn held out the crook of her arm and said, "Shall we."

Craig took it and they went through the small ship. After Craig had shown her around, marveling at the subtle differences in decor except for the control room, he indicated the learning chair and helmet. For the first time since the start of the tour, Ship said, "I think that you let Dawn have an introduction from me. If you don't mind. Dawn, would you sit in the chair and pull the helmet down." Craig helped her and then sat back in another console chair to watch her. The session only lasted five minutes.

Wide-eyed Dawn emerged from the learning chair. "Craig. That was amazing. Ship explained that only you can get the full knowledge of ship as the chosen one, but now I fully understand the history and your mission. I'm yours to command. What do we do next?" Craig and Dawn spent the next several hours on the sofa in the living room area with its curving window to space and discussed possible plans.

After many of the issues that Craig had wanted to talk about and after answering many of Dawn's questions, their nearness started to tell on each other. They had made love in weightlessness again, and in the bed, and on the sofa, and back in bed again with serious discussions in between until Ship awakened them from the bed, with "Craig, your meetings start in thirty minutes."

16 PLANNING

"Dawn, I have a very critical meeting in thirty minutes at the Engineering Building conference room with all of the professors and some visitors from other places. I think you should also attend. I would like your input during and after. Do you mind?"

"Of course not, Craig. But what do I wear?"

Ship broke in, "Sorry, clothing is still not allowed for duel transport. I suggest that I send you back to your sorority. Craig can come back here and get dressed."

Craig said, "Ready?" Dawn nodded. They hugged; they appeared on her bed at the sorority. "I'll pick you up outside in 15 minutes, okay?"

"No. You need to get there. Why don't you teleport to the ship and then to the meeting. I'll make my grand entrance later. Okay?" Craig gave her a long kiss and zapped.

There were experts from around the country and Representative Shea. Introductions were made and the discussions began. Craig seemed distracted until the door opened at 10:00 AM sharp and Dawn walked in wearing a severe business suit with knee length skirt, heels and tucked in white scarf. Gentlemen, "I would like you to meet my assistant, Dawn."

Dawn broke in, "Dawn Weathers as in forecasting. Craig asked me to attend because of my presentation on Astral Navigation. I am here to present the real problem that Craig has not told you all yet. If I may." She looked at Craig.

"Certainly. I am really glad you could make it." Dawn had spent the two hours she was late preparing a computer based briefing with graphic pictures and some simulations of the approximate course of the asteroid that would strike the Earth, the timing, and then a run down on the effects of the asteroid strike.

"As you can see gentlemen, if it strikes the earth, it will create a crater nearly two hundred miles in diameter forming either a new inland sea or dramatically changing the coastline somewhere. If it were to strike in the mountains, there would be no water filling in the hole, and the explosion could be somewhat shielded from populated areas. If not in the mountains, the explosive force would destroy any man made structure within five hundred miles from the strike and even at eight hundred miles only a steel reinforced concrete bunker would survive. The earthquakes resulting from the strike would carry through to the other side of the earth destroying hundreds of miles of mankind opposite the strike with destruction lessening in concentric circles away from the main destructive zones. If it hit in the central part of the United States, only the west coast would maybe survive, but the earthquakes even there would destroy most of the man made structures. There is some possibility that some buildings might survive in Europe, South America, Africa and the eastern part of the Soviet Union. The dust raised would be the most serious problem assuming you survived the strike. The Earth will be covered with a three to six inch layer of powder fine dust. This will bury all grasses and suffocate many trees. Any small animals will suffocate. The only food available after the first month would be stored food. This dust will fall for approximately three months and will block thirty to fifty percent of the sunlight for most of this period. There will be increased dust in the atmosphere for three to ten years lowering the temperature of the earth dramatically. Every point on earth would cool by eighty degrees for most of this period. There might be some areas around the equator that could still be livable, but that is assuming that the Earth's rotation stays the same. Remember, it was a similar event that destroyed the dinosaurs, even at the equator. It could slow the rotation of Earth to the point that one side cooks while the other actually has frozen gases. It could wobble the Earth out of its orbit and send it toward…or away from the sun. Either would end all higher life. A strike in the ocean would be less severe. If it struck in the Pacific the tidal waves would exceed over one thousand feet high and six hundred miles an hour by the time it hit land on either side of the ocean. All islands including Japan and the Philippines would be washed clean. The tidal wave on the America's west coast would destroy all life west of the mountains on both North and South America. Eighty percent of all life in China would disappear. There would be no dust, but the water in the air would create a similar cooling effect to the dust buy would not last as long. There would be world wide snow and rainstorms that would destroy most life anywhere. The cooling would not be as severe due to the fact that most of the water would return to Earth within a month. Imagine every stream and river at twice the height of the worst recorded flood. Within a week the rain would change to snow even at the equator covering everything with feet of snow. There would also be a reduced possibility of changing the Earth's orbit, but how many plants and animals could survive six months of ten foot deep snow. It may have been a similar event that caused Noah to launch his ark. Yes, there is evidence that there was a great flood in our history. The story of Noah could be true. What of the story of Atlantis? That may also be true. Remember the Mammoths that died eating grasses in Canada and Siberia? Mankind may survive in small numbers. Apparently this kind of event is not all that uncommon. How would a few thousand survivors fair with no modern tools or industry? Does that explain the peaks and valleys of prehistoric man that may have been around for two million years?"

Showing photographs of Mars, she showed them the 2,500-mile-long Valles Marineris rift. "Gentlemen. That is possibly created by an asteroid strike. It could have blown off most of the atmosphere of Mars. I have presented a scenario, but my main purpose here is to provide for astral navigation once you build your spaceships to the stars."

After a few moments of silence, Mr. Scoffed spoke up. "I don't doubt the science here, but I have a question. Is there any possibility that we could use nuclear bombs in space to deflect this asteroid?"

Dawn answered, "The make up of this asteroid may be a primordial metal composition. Remember I said the size is forty to 100 miles in diameter. You may be able to blow off a few chunks, but I doubt that you could change its course. Keep in mind this could sink Atlantis if it existed or Australia. How many nuclear bombs would it take to sink Australia? That could be a backup plan. If you could start exploding nuclear bombs on one side at one hundred thousand miles or more out and keep them coming…you might be able to cause enough deflection, but I would rather be on my way elsewhere. However, Craig and I were discussing the situation yesterday and we came to the conclusion that at the best we might be able to evacuate one million people leaving the other four billion to die. So everything is worth considering."

Representative Shea said, "Gentlemen. I suggest that we take a break for lunch and come back at two. Let's keep everything you have heard here top secret. I don't want one word outside of this room. Craig, I want to talk to you, now!"

When the others had left, he continued to Craig and Dawn that had refused to leave, "Craig, why did you keep this a secret for almost a year?

My God! You were right. There is nothing more important on this Earth. I want to recommend that we make this international. I don't just mean your invited scientists. We must get governments involved, and the sooner the better. Again, why did you keep this a secret? What else are you keeping secret?"

"Sir, no one would have believed me if a college sophomore started spouting off. I had to prove myself to some key people first. Do you think I could have gotten this many key scientists together in one place to even discuss this last year? No one knew who I was. They still don't know half of it. You wouldn't believe me if I tried to tell you all of it now."

"Well?"

"Would you believe that I get my knowledge from Atlantis?"

"No."

"Okay, then. Just attend the rest of this week long session, and then make your assessment. Last week, you would not have listened to me. I did not want to keep secrets, but I have had to until the time was right. Let's let the scientists give their opinion on who should know about the end of the world. I think the average person that knew they only had a few years left to live might go kind of crazy. You could not control the crime and drugs. People would quit working. Without everyone working, there is no hope to build ships for anyone to survive."

That afternoon, that floor of the building was closed off except for the stairwell. Representative Shea had called in the local FBI that had called the Oklahoma State Bureau of Investigation (OSBI) that had called in state troopers. There were guards around the building and students and professors just attending normal classes had to show their identification to get close to the building. The local television stations were stationed around campus corner. The FBI itself controlled access to that floor of the building. Any other classes on that floor were moved to other classrooms on campus. By Tuesday evening CNN was doing specials on something happening at the University of Oklahoma and NBC, ABC, and CBS were doing stories on the history of the University, the state, the football team, the colleges represented on campus, the other universities in Oklahoma. The secure cordon expanded to a block around the Engineering Building. Students were protesting the disruption of their classrooms. You have to understand the University of Oklahoma students. There were no big protests or rioting. When winning a national championship in college football, only about 25% of the students attended the rally to honor the team. In equal number were families with their young children. The team did most of the shouting, not the crowd. On Wednesday, the media circus moved to the Cowboy Hall of Fame in Oklahoma City that was easier to secure, but then the FBI got nervous about the view from the highway and had the conference moved to the Kilpatrick Center that could be totally closed off and was not near any major highways. The logistics caused problems because of the lack of lodging near the Kilpatrick Center, and the FBI was now nervous about the empty expanses of the Lincoln Zoo next door. It was only a few blocks from Interstate 35. The meeting was called off and another meeting was scheduled for six weeks later in the Pentagon where the FBI and military could guarantee security.

Each evening when the meeting broke up, Dawn and Craig had gone back to Ship, the hard way. Dawn had gone to her room and Craig to his and then Craig appeared in Dawn's room, undressed the two of them and zapped back to the Ship for love making. Craig rented an apartment near the university on Tuesday during the lunch break and Dawn had gone by after the meeting and bought furniture for it. This simplified things and eliminated the need to go to the ship at night. Now they could drive to the apartment together in one car and spend the night together right there. They were not as comfortable there as in the ship, and they had to either cook their own meals or eat out, but it was definitely more normal. Now that the meetings had broken up on Thursday at noon, a day and a half early, Craig and Dawn decided to go to the ship where they would have privacy to talk about the meeting without having to worry about thin walls

17 MARRIAGE PLANS

"Craig. There is one thing I have to tell you. My parents will find out that I have moved in with a man and out of the sorority soon if they don't already know. It will come as a pretty severe shock to them, especially considering my life over the past several years. I haven't dated much because of my studies and now the university will be coming after us for living off campus without being 21. I will have to explain something to them. I know you, I love you, but I know nothing about you to even tell them about you. I haven't called them in a week. What am I going to say to them?"

"Dawn. You are right of course. I have not talked to my parents much for the last year. I have not told them about Ship. The fact that we are living together would be a shock to them, even if I am a boy. If I were a girl, they would just about disown me. I do understand what you are saying."

"Of course. I don't have a choice. I can't live with you without getting married. I can't even go to the ship with you unless we go without clothes. I would say that tends to lead to things that are supposed to go with marriage. We will be working together for many years into the future. However, in the Episcopal church we are supposed to go to pre-marriage counseling with the priest."

Dawn, "I don't know what to make of anything. I do love you, but I'm not sure about a formal marriage. I hope you don't take this wrong, but I don't really know you that well. I thought I was in love with another a few weeks ago. I don't think I'm ready for marriage. I don't want to lose you, but I'm not sure if it's love or your knowledge that I need. It wouldn't be right to be married. Ship said we were married… I'm confused. I liked your priest or minister or whatever you call him in the Episcopal Church when I met him last Sunday. Do you realize it's only been a week?"

"Yes, Craig. I do realize that. We will be partners for now. I know you need my knowledge. For some reason, Ship seems to be very deficient in navigation. Maybe the Atlanteans were too wrapped up in technology to the point that they trusted the computer and not their own intellect. The mission needs me because we cannot duplicate the Ship and we will have to rely on human navigators in space. Can we confide in Father Joe?"

"We could teleport in on him and ask. Can we trust him to keep the silence? Will he believe us?"

"We can trust him. I think between us he might believe us. He will at least listen honestly to us. We can't teleport in on him. Don't you remember how we have to transport?"

"Ooooh. I see your point. You don't just pop in on a priest naked, do you. Well, I could pop in and ask him to meet with us somewhere soon. My teleporting in on him should stress the importance. We need to do this fast."

"I don't know, Craig. I mean, I'm sure he wouldn't mind, but what about my parents? They are going to want us married. We need to talk with them somehow. We can't just keep living together."

"Do we have time for that?"

"Craig, I think we need to do something. Why not drop in on my parents? We can zap to my bedroom at my house. You can zap back and get some clothing and then I'll meet you in the front yard, and we can ring the doorbell like a conventional girl and boy friend coming home to meet parents. We can ask them about it. They are my parents."

"Since you don't know about me, I will answer the questions about myself that you can't, okay. I think that would be a good idea. We don't have anything to do right now, ready?"

It took two hours before they were ready to go visit her parents and they had not talked much, but at last they were ready. Craig showed Dawn how they could watch a monitor in the control room as Ship showed them what was happening at their house. Her father was saying, "Martha, I say right now that we had better go to the university tomorrow after work and find out what our daughter is doing. That letter you are holding makes it sound like the whole last year has been strange. This last week she has disappeared out of her sorority and skipped classes all week. That is not like her. I would have called the police except the dorm mother says that she is living with some guy, at least according to her friends."

"Let's not wait, Craig." It took Dawn twenty minutes to get dressed and to sneak out to the front yard to meet Craig. He had the Viper sitting in the driveway.

"Where did you get the car?"

"I had Ship put one out for me to impress your parents if they looked. They might ask how we got here you know. By the way, I didn't think of it earlier, but as long as it is only on the Earth, ship can teleport any one person from one point to another…just not to the ship...and not with clothing. I am the only one that can take things with me, and you know how I have to take a person with me."

"Is the car legal? Ship can do that?"

"Yes, Ship can produce anything in limited quantities. Actually excess quantities for twenty people for hundreds of years, but forget hundreds or thousands of people. It just couldn't keep up then. I don't know if it's legal. There are no matching registrations. It was not manufactured by Chrysler."

"Dawn? Is that you?" Her dad said.

"Yes, Daddy, it's me. I've got some exciting news for you."

"Well, I've wanted to talk with you too. Come on in. Who's this with you?"

"This is Craig Decker, Daddy. I brought him home to meet you and to discuss our plans."

"Take your coats? Go have a seat in the living room there. Martha, this is Craig Decker."

"Hello." She said coldly.

After the got seated, it was obviously up to Dawn to start the conversation. "Mom, Dad. Craig and I want your advice and help."

"How long have you known him and how long have you been going together?" Her mother asked.

Her father cut in, "That's quite a car you have there. It must have cost around a hundred grand. Are you from a wealthy family?"

Craig saved Dawn who didn't know, "No. You may know my father; he was the Oklahoma teacher of the year in 1971. He's retired now, but everyone around Enid used to know him. The rest of the family settled around Seiling during the land rush."

Mr. Weather asked, "How did a school teacher afford to buy a car like that?"

"Oh it's mine. Maybe you heard about me winning the Texas lottery. I have anything I want now that I have my PhD's. Maybe you've seen me on the news. At any rate, Mrs. Weather, Dawn and I have known each other most of the year, but we just made the decision last weekend. That's why we decided that we needed to consult with you. You probably saw the news about the meeting at OU this last week, your daughter was the star. Because of the subject of those meetings we will need to be together constantly for next several years, to the point that last Sunday, we decided to make it ourselves a permanent partnership."

"Are you pregnant?" Mrs. Weather asked.

"No, Mom, I am not pregnant, in fact, that is not a current consideration. It's just that what Craig said is correct. We can't tell you what it is about, but we are the leaders of the team. Actually, Craig is the leader. I'm just his partner and counselor. At any rate, we are leading the most massive research and production project the world has known in modern times. We will have to travel together, work together, and essentially sleep together for the next nine years or more. Wait Dad. This will be far more important than any official degrees that I might get. In a few years you will know what we were doing that was so important. Yes, we love each other. Yes, it would be nice to get married, but we have already had to start living together for the project, and I want to be married, but Craig has reservations?"

"If it helps, I haven't even had a chance to talk with my parents in months. I haven't told Dawn yet, but next week Princeton is going to award her the first doctorate degree in astral navigation and a major grant. In fact, if she agrees, she will have to take some of her time over the next few years teaching astral navigation to a new class of astronauts as the first full professor of a new degree program."

Dawn looked at him incredulously, "Why haven't you told me? But will I have time to teach classes? That's marvelous, but…"

"Yes, Dawn, you will have time. By next fall, the rest of the team should be able to take more of the leadership. Besides, you know the importance of that new degree program more than I do."

Her father slapped his knees loudly and said, "That's it then. Martha, I would say you have a lot of work to do. Dawn, you and your mother will go out tomorrow and buy a wedding gown, arrange for a cake, and get invitations printed. I will have my office address them this week. What day do you want to get married?"

"Dad, I'm so happy you agree. I would like to get married in Saint Johns in Norman. We want to make it very quick, but we haven't talked with the minister yet. Mom, how long do we need to get ready?"

"Well, your Dad's for it. I don't know if I am or not. It's too quick. Your life is going too quick. I'm glad you decided to get married rather than just live together. Two weeks would be nice. Everyone will wonder, but we can get everything done by then. You had better talk with your minister before we get the invitations printed. If you are going to go this quickly, then maybe you and, uh, Craig is it? Well you had better go tell his parents and talk with the minister. I know your father, Craig. He was well respected around here. I had him for a teacher myself once. I hope you have some of what he had. Okay, Dawn, Craig, if your Dad's for it, then I'm for it. Are you going to spend the night here?"

"If that's okay, Mom, Dad. We need to go get over to tell Craig's parents and then he will drive me back here for the night, but we can only afford a few hours tomorrow."

When they got in the car to go to Craig's house, Craig responded, "Dawn. I said I was not ready to get married. I may not be in love."

"Craig. Lot's of people get married for convenience. The Earth needs us as partners now. It's bad enough that our parents will surely die when the asteroids arrive. Can't we leave them thinking that we are happily married?"

"But Dawn, I'm not ready for marriage. Maybe I don't have a choice as far as the ship is concerned, but I thought I was in love with another last week. I've known her for awhile now too. She really thinks she loves me. Last time I saw her we did not have sex because I was so attracted to her that I was afraid I would forget about the mission."

"Craig, let's just call it a marriage for convenience. It doesn't have to be that public. We can keep it out of the news. Once the mission is assured, we can separate if you still don't want marriage."

Craig and Dawn drove to Craig's house where the same scenario was played out.

Again Craig tried, "Dawn. I really don't know. I respect you a lot. I know the mission needs you. I don't know."

"Craig. No choice. Marriage or we go our separate ways and Earth dies."

After Craig dropped Dawn off at her house, he zapped into the Episcopal priest's home where he caught him working alone on the next week's sermon.

"Excuse me."

"I remember your name, Craig isn't it. Did my wife let you in?"

"No sir, I teleported in. Now don't get scared. I am going to disappear and reappear in that chair over there. Okay?"

"See. Here I am. I can't tell you what is going on. All I can saw is that Dawn Weather and I are teamed up for the next many many years working on the most important project to save lives that has been undertaken since Christ died on the cross. I don't mean to be sacrilegious, but this is that important. I can teleport across the United States quicker than you can dial the telephone. You came from back east. If you need proof, give me their address back east and I will be there in their house to answer the telephone. It's part of the technology. You must believe me that we are working to save the human race from extinction. We can only save a few. We are very short on time, we must start living together on the project, and we both want to get married immediately or sooner. You know Dawn. I was not raised in the Episcopal Church, but I know everything there is to know about it recorded in history. You could ask me anything and I could answer it better than your bishops. I know that I need Dawn and she wants to be with me. Our parents have agreed to us getting married, but do not know about our project. How soon can you marry us?"

"Woah. Slow down son. That is simply amazing. I believe you, but I am required to give you counseling before marriage. I don't feel that quick marriages can last. How do you feel about divorce?"

"I don't believe in divorce, but we feel that we should be married due to the fact that we will have to living together, possibly the rest of our lives. Right now, at least, we need to get married for our parents, for appearances, for our reputations, or the good of Earth. You know about me, I've become famous. You already knew Dawn. We have known each other for several months although not closely except for a week or so. Dawn and I led the meetings this week that brought in all the police. We will have to be living together for years to come. Dawn wants to get married in your church. We can attend twice this week if you want. Next Saturday, the week after?"

"To test your story, even though you apparently disappeared in front of me, I'm going to dial the number of a male cousin that was born on the same day I was. Will you answer the telephone?"

"Yes. If your cousin is there I will let you speak to him." Craig disappeared and ten seconds later answered the telephone on the first ring.

"Father Joe. I'm here. Ted, the telephone is for you."

Ted walked in, saw Craig, stopped and said, "Who are you?"

"Your cousin, Father Joe, will tell you. Do you want to speak to him?"

"Yes." As Ted answered the telephone, Craig disappeared and reappeared in Father Joe's room.

"Ted, don't worry. The man you saw is not there. He's here. Someday, maybe I can explain to you. I'm still a priest and I have not sinned. Trust me. Yes, next time we see each other, I'll tell you what I know." Father Joe hung up the telephone.

"Okay, let's say that there is more here than I can understand. Let's say that what you say is true. Why do you have to get married?"

"Because we are going to be living together."

"Do you have to live together? Why can't you live separately and just work together?"

"Sir. That will be impossible. We may even be isolated from everyone for weeks at a time."

"I will need to talk with Dawn privately and then with both of you. I will write it down for Saturday after next. But you have to promise me that you will meet with me three times before then. Agreed?"

"Thank you sir."

Craig appeared in Dawn's bedroom and they both teleported to the ship where they could talk. "Well, we are set to get married in two weeks. We have to meet with your priest three times. He wants to talk with you alone next. I said Monday afternoon at 5 o'clock. I will meet with him at 7 o'clock. Tuesday we meet with him together at 5 and Thursday, same time."

"That's great, Craig. You've made my whole life for me. However, we have some serious discussions. Let's review what happened this week during the meetings."

18 HISTORY LESSON

"That can wait for tomorrow. Let's …" He took her back to her bedroom at 6 o'clock the next morning. She got dressed and went to wake her parents. Craig went to talk with his parents again. Saturday afternoon, Craig picked Dawn up to go back, ostensibly to talk with her Episcopal minister, but instead, they drove to a private spot. They undressed, zapped to the ship and had the car zapped into storage as if it had never existed.

Dawn made them review the meeting this time. "Okay, the consensus was there were too many ifs, but if everything falls into place, we can get maybe 1,000 ships built. If the journey to another planet takes ten years, then each can take 1,000 people and recycle enough food for that period of time. If the journey is one year, then each ship could take 5,000. If the journey takes 20 years than only 500 per ship. The first ship hull can be completed in 3 years. If an engine and fuel can be developed to launch it, they can use it as an orbital base to outfit it and supply it in space. That will take another 2 years. They can then use it as a base to build another in space and then both can be used to build two more. Why can't you give them the teleportation secret?"

"I wish I could, but we are nearly 100 years behind where we should have been due to my predecessors' personal greed for fame and fortune.

Some of them simply fell in love with the wrong woman and forgot their mission. They didn't feel the urgency when it was 1,000 years in the future. At 100 years in the future, there was still that problem. Now. Well, you understand the urgency, and I understand the danger of falling for the wrong woman. Thank God, I came to get you that Sunday morning last week."

"I take it you have other girl friends."

"Not now. Last week. Not now. We are getting married in two weeks and I will never betray your trust. I take marriage very seriously. You made me mad, which was good. I brought you to the ship who confirmed that I had chosen right, and now we are a team. You are the best choice I had once I realized it."

"Then Ship didn't make the decision you did?"

"Yes. I made the choice. Ship didn't help at all, if anything Ship confused me for several months by recommending others. Once I chose you, Ship just confirmed that you were the best choice I could have made. Don't thank Ship or blame Ship. Ship definitely did not help, but the confusion Ship introduced helped me make the right decision. I still want to marry you and it will be for life. As if there was ever a choice for either of us. It was predestined from the start."

"Thanks, Craig. I feel better now. At any rate we can save a million at best. Maybe only 500,000. If we could make it a short trip we could save 5 million. Regardless. Most of the human race will be left behind. How do we pick? Will the rich and famous buy their passage? Will we select a super race like the Nazis tried to? Ship, jump in here with your opinion at any time. How do we select who goes and who does not?"

Ship said, *"Money and power is meaningless to this venture. I would recommend good breeders. I would also recommend a ratio of ten women for each man to produce more people to colonize more places."*

"Excuse me Ship! What's this about ten women to each man and colonizing more places?"

"Well, it should be obvious that you would not want to trust one unknown planet to put all of mankind. That's what the Atlanteans did when they moved to Earth from Mars."

"Wait. Moved from Mars?"

"Yes. Didn't Craig tell you? Mankind started on Mars, but with the cooling of the sun and the low atmosphere of Mars, Earth seemed much more inviting. I know you know about the pyramids and other artifacts on Mars. You have seen them yourself. Craig had not, but you have. You should also know about the semi-permanent settlement on the moon while the Atlanteans waited to pacify what you call Atlantis. They actually generated a breathable atmosphere on the moon for twenty years while they moved the indigenous cavemen off the continent and then built cities for the main population on Mars. The Atlanteans as you know them only lived here for 50,000 years before permanently leaving for other solar systems. There were forty million that moved out of this solar system and another forty million chose to stay on Earth and try to survive without their modern civilization. Some moved to Egypt and were known as the builders. Actually they built many of your ancient civilizations. I helped them advance their culture again, but they never regained space travel. Most of them died off through a combination of interbreeding and diseases without their technology. When they left here they left in all directions. Their intention was to take plenty of women along for breeding new civilizations on new planets. When you have ships with 1,000 per ship, there is a good possibility that one ship will land on a planet by itself. With 500 men and 500 women could only produce 500 children per year or only 5000 at the end of 10 years. You should keep in mind that women breathe less oxygen and eat less than men so an extended voyage is better with fewer men. The Mormons knew that when they went west. It works." With only 100 men you could have 1200 women or 1300 per ship in the same amount of space, breathing the same amount of air and eating the same amount of food, they could expand their population by 900 per year. In ten years they will have 10 times as many people, and still only 10,000 to tame an entire planet."

"Okay, Ship. We get your point. However we select our crews for the voyage, we need to have a high ratio of women to men if we want to conquer planets and we can save more of mankind with the same amount of ships. Is there any way that we could somehow invent a portion or your capability of producing food from mass or converting mass to energy and back like you do?"

"No. Your technology is actually 300 years behind the minimum planned for your time. However, you nearly have the capability of having controlled fusion. With controlled fusion you can produce tremendous amounts of energy and with energy you can travel faster than with your proposed ion drives and produce enough energy to develop a nearly self regenerating food supply with hydroponics. I do not know what kind of ships you will be able to produce because I have not had dedicated people that took my suggestions through. While your wars have helped by speeding your own development it has also caused your technology to drift. Corruption has caused your development to sometimes stagnate. For example. At the end of WWII you developed the flying wing which could have lead to designs more suited for space travel, but then you drifted back to building airplanes with inefficient fuselage and wing arrangements that should have been abandoned. Your nuclear power development was commendable once WWII was over, but then you had an arms race with the Soviet Union that set both countries back in nuclear development. Then you had people that demonstrated against nuclear energy development even though proved safe compared to all other forms of energy. Rather than explore near space and finding the previous evidence of space faring predecessors, you built missiles to point at each other. Your oil and coal companies selfishly kept trying to force civilization to continue using these polluting fuels. You should have developed breeder reactors before 1960, but stagnated. All of your factories and transportation could have used electricity with no pollution from nuclear reactors. Your homes should have been heated by electricity instead of coal and oil. In Oklahoma and Texas where there was plenty of clean burning natural gas for generating electricity, but the coal companies got a law passed to require a certain percentage be produced from coal. Need I go on?"

"No, Ship. Again, we have your point. What should I do to help the development of this new fusion nuclear power plant?"

"Sit in the learning chair."

"Later. Dawn and I need to discuss the meeting more right now. Dawn, what do you think about the crew makeup?"

"I agree with Ship. I had not thought about it, but it does make sense about the higher proportion of women. However, that in itself can create problems. Men still run this world and a lot of these men would be stupid, sorry, but many men would be selfish enough to have a higher number of men than women. The first colonists to the New World were mainly men. Many of the Spanish brought no women, but mated with native women. I would presume that there will be no native women on an alien planet. It was only after they established a colony that they then brought women, and many of these women were women of ill repute or that could not get a man to marry them in Europe. This was a poor way to get breeding stock from a scientific standpoint. For this expedition, we won't need brute strength as much as we need numbers, like Ship said. Women are just as smart as men and we need two things, brains and numbers. The women should be picked based upon their intelligence and crews made up primarily with women that meet certain educational requirements to assure that each ship has redundant knowledge in all areas. To prevent the women from fighting over the men, we technically should eliminate the men and bring along frozen sperm. Counter opinions?"

"I agree with Ship also, but I think you are going too far. Men have a few talents also. For one thing, we don't know about these new worlds. Yes, we can bring along some equipment with us, but there still needs to be a man's strength for some of the jobs on the new world. Men think differently than women. There are circumstances where men generally have better thinking capability. We don't know if we will find worlds that are totally friendly. If there are creatures capable of eating people, such as our bears and mountain lions, men do kill better and plan defenses and offenses better. We were brought up to be physically competitive for a reason. There needs to be some fighters. Also, you cannot select the crews just on mental capability. I don't want to sound like a Nazi, but you pointed out yourself about how women were picked wrong for the New World. The women should definitely be picked on their mental capabilities, but should also be picked for their child bearing capability, physical fitness with the men being picked for sperm count, physical fitness, and mental capabilities. However, not all mental capability is measured by formal education. You need mechanics. Women don't make good mechanics and men that are educated are frequently not the best mechanics. Each ship needs mechanics, whether for repairing a surface vehicle or nuclear reactor. Women make good programmers, but men are better at assembling or even inventing new computers. Traditionally, men have been the providers while the women were bearing children. A ship that only had 100 men and 1000 pregnant women would not be well suited for chopping down a forest to build houses and plant crops. That brings up another point. We don't really know how long this voyage will be. If the women were all 25 years old at launch, the ship is maxed out for people and the voyage takes 15 years…all of the women will be past child bearing age when they arrive. We have to prepare to have a generation of children born on board ships unless we can find out how to get people there quickly. We don't know where."

"Well, Craig, are we back to 500 men and 500 women?"

"No, Dawn. How about a compromise? You and I need to find a planet that we can aim for and then see where our technology is so we will know how long the voyage will be. I suspect that more women than men is good, but let's make sure that we have enough men. We should tentatively plan on some children being born in route. The natural state of things is to have a 50/50 mix of men to women. One for one. Monogamous marriages and all that. I don't think we can make the final decision yet until we know more. If you agree let's go on with an inventory of what each ship needs."

"I guess the women's lib stuff got me going a little. I know that I would not want to go exploring a new planet without you along to protect me. Yes, I can shoot a gun, but I don't know if I could kill a deer. If attacked by an animal, I might panic first, and shoot too late. You're right about the mechanics too. Matter of fact, if you look at inventions in history, very few were made by women. However, women are better at making things. Men invent or create something new from nothing, but when it comes to making many, women produce more. It takes both men and women. I agree that we will have to wait to make a decision. The decision isn't just ours either. I do think we should start talking about a high proportion of women in the crew. Speaking of physically fit and suited for child bearing or fathering, I have been thinking of white European decent people. In reality, we should be looking at multiple races of people. I am prejudiced, but I intellectually know I shouldn't be. How many Chinese, Japanese, Blacks, Mexicans? How do we choose? Who does the choosing?

"Good point. When it comes to the Chinese, Japanese, French, Germans, Russians, there is little doubt about who they will choose. Africa will never have the money to launch their own ships. The Arabs will have the money, but what about the technology. They treat women as property, so their women will not be as productive for anything except producing children. If those first countries cannot produce enough for their own people, they will not let the Arabs have any. Smaller countries like Thailand, the Philippines, New Zealand, and other small countries will loose their representation. Mexico might have one or two ships, but will the Mexican Americans not be represented in our ships. How about the Blacks? If our ship only ended up with 100 people would we have 1 male and 9 female Blacks to make up the 10% of Blacks in America? What if the male died? Mexicans? Vietnamese? What about the other minorities in the United States? Will the Dutch be represented? Will they take along their share of Blacks that live in Holland? The Swiss. Can we get all of these ethnic groups to be properly represented? Will they all settle on one planet without starting up new ethnic wars? Do the Vikings take all men and plan on conquering other groups with few men to take their women like the Vikings of old? This could go on and on. Obviously, our US ships will have to have the proper portion of ethnic groups or selection criteria that assure the ones we want are on board. Secrecy in all of this must be maintained, and yet you and I have the responsibility to solve as much of this as possible."

"Craig, that's a horrible thought. What if the Chinese, Japanese, Arabs, and others with a bias against women take all male crews and weapons with the idea of conquering the Europeans that take mainly women and agricultural equipment instead of weapons? Do we try to find separate planets for these different groups to make sure that they don't try something like this?"

"Well, we do have a monopoly on the technology right now. There is not much time before the catastrophe. If we could keep the secrets, we could build all of the ships and then sell space on them to assure that the crew and cargo are to our liking. Maybe we could get all of the other countries to produce the day to day stuff and convert our industry to ship building. We would trade ship space for the goods of the other countries. I really don't know. I don't know who we can talk to about it except you, me, and Ship. You know that if Congress pays, they expect to have the say so and save themselves first. Then the corporate heads of the companies will want their families. The rich will have their dues."

"Craig. That's terrible. True, but terrible. You're right of course. Those that have the most to do with the financing of the ships will have their families on board regardless of what makes sense. Ship, you can just in here at any time now."

"My programming did not fully appreciate this problem you are posing. The Atlanteans had no such problems. They had enough ships that anyone that wanted to go could go. That will not be the case here. The Atlanteans were so far advanced over the indigenous humanoids, that they never considered offering space to Egyptians or Greeks or others. Theirs was the only technology and everything was owned by everyone or at least in my programming. Of course, I am beginning to understand why so many Atlanteans simply escaped to the other continents and got left behind. I know there were priests. I know there were elite groups. My programming is flawed. I don't know if I can help. My programming says 1 man for each 10 women, but I did not consider some ships from other countries carrying all men to conquer others. Maybe that is why the Atlanteans fled in all directions rather than all going to one planet. Maybe when some came here from Mars, maybe others went elsewhere instead of Earth. I just cannot tell you unless you stick to my programming."

"Dawn. I have a unique extended family of cousins. There were 33 of us and 32 went to college. We used to get together when we were younger and discuss zany ideas like this. Why don't we have a pre-wedding party to discuss this? I can arrange for airfare for all of them."

"I hardly know my cousins. I wouldn't think of asking them. If you think it might help, do it."

They made an inventory of what was needed for the evacuation ships.

1. The new metal would make the hulls and interior walls. It would generally protect the occupants from meteors and other smaller objects, but each bulkhead inside would have to be equipped with self sealing doors that the onboard computer would close in case of a hull breach. Each ship would look like a flying wing and would use a rocket booster to fly into space from the ground. Each ship would orbit their world until the found a suitable landing area and then do a dead stick landing with no runway. Each ship would be 200 feet long with a 300 foot wingspan with an average thickness of 30 feet.

2. Power would be provided by a controlled fusion reactor. The new metal would totally block radiation protecting the crew from both exterior and reactor radiation. This would dramatically reduce the size of the nuclear power plant. The main drive would have to be nuclear, because no other fuel would provide the long term acceleration required. By using fusion, the amount of fuel would be reduced. Technically they could start throwing in used food containers for fuel if need be. There would be no anti-gravity so the acceleration would have to be limited to what the crew could take for long periods of time. Once the ship was in space, they would use nuclear power exclusively. They would begin with a 12 hour burn building to an acceleration of two gees at the end of the first six hours with everyone strapped in or laying on swivel couches. The acceleration would be reduced to 1 gee for the remainder of the trip. At that acceleration light speed would be reached in six months and another six months required stopping at the destination. With continuous

acceleration they would exceed the speed of light and they could go almost anywhere in the galaxy in five or six years.

3. The amount of food would be prodigious. If each person required 2 pounds of food per day and if you assumed that 20 pounds took one cubic foot and each person had 800 cubic feet to play around in (10X10X8 feet) to include recreation areas, hallways, etc. This would mean rooms that are only 8X8X8 for each person. This mandates a high proportion of female to males because females need less space than males. If you can picture a family of 4 living in a 500 square foot small 1 bedroom apartment with no possibility of going outside for 5 years, you have the idea. The hydroponics area will produce additional food and convert carbon dioxide into oxygen. This will also provide an open area to relieve claustrophobia. We will have to test the entire crew for claustrophobia. All wastes will be reprocessed into fresh water, fertilizer or fed to the reactor for fusion material. The presumed water lost from all sources is 4 ounces per person per day.

4. All equipment will be packed as assemblies to be assembled on landing. There will be one bulldozer to plow out rough roads and fields. There must be farm equipment. Each person will require hand tools ranging from pick and tree axes to cookware and eating plates. There will be some generalized manufacturing equipment, to include kilns for smelting metals on location. This will be a paperless operation. No books, no communications with home, just stored information from the computer. There will be a limited number of vehicles for exploration, transport of larger items, and any people that are not totally ambulatory. Each person will have hand weapons available in case of indigenous animal threats. By weapons I mean hand guns and a limited number of high power rifles. A few of the men will also have access to a very limited number of heavier weapons that should work against all but the largest dinosaurs. All motorized equipment will run on batteries or wired directly to the ship.

5. The ship will be the principle residence of the crew after landing until more permanent quarters can be built.

6. The light aircraft are to explore the land area of hundreds of miles around the new settlements for whatever was not spotted from space during the weeks of orbit before landing.

7. Each country will have its own planet, continental mass, or large area for its own, depending on what has been discovered before launch date. Within the first year of launch the landing location could be changed, but in general there will be few course corrections after launch.

After they completed this list, Craig commented, "Well, the only technology truly just missing is the fusion power plant and a way to fuel it. If people eat 2 pounds of food per day and there are 1000 people on board, that is 2000 pounds of potential fusion fuel + most of the 4 ounces of water lost per person per day."

Dawn replied, "If we assume we can get the powers to approve a woman to man mixture of 8 to 1. We could transport 1400 people per ship. If we increase the men we have to increase the food used and space per person needed. If we make the ratio 1 to 1, then the maximum is 1050. Each ship can carry 350 extra people with the higher ratio. Note, Craig, I admit that we need the men. I would also carry some amount of frozen sperm to diversify the genetics more. It would not be good to have so many half brothers and sisters getting married. We might prevent any of that through rules, but it would not take long before it was cousins or second cousins marrying."

"Dawn, not to put pressure on you, but astral navigation over 10 to 200 light years is going to be critical. Assuming we could find planets for the expedition, the Ship will store coordinates and courses. What about our new ships without the computer power of Ship. We will be relying on astronomers and astral navigators to know where they are and if they are on course. If they miss by a few million miles, they will have to find their way to their destination in a new part of the galaxy. Might be interesting.

19 WEDDING BELLS

They never got around to discussing the other issues from the meeting because this one was so critical and the wedding was so soon. The meeting of the cousins was inconclusive although unbiased and interesting. Suggestions ranged from plan on taking only a few people, to make the technology freely available to everyone, to find investors that will provide the money out of altruism and let you pick the crew. It was fun and Dawn enjoyed meeting the interesting family of college graduates. The wedding preparations were rushed, but it worked.

The wedding was short and sweet with only their parents and some of Craig's cousins that lived nearby. The wedding was like an arrange wedding or a wedding of convenience. It made the parents comfortable with Dawn and Craig living together and being together 24/7 palpable. Were either one in love…probably not in such a short time.

20 HONEYMOON ON THE MOON

After they drove away from the wedding in Craig's Viper Craig asked, "We have been so busy we didn't discuss what we are going to do for a honeymoon. I have tickets and hotel reservations for Hawaii. Sound good to you?"

"No, I was thinking about the moon and Mars to try out the ship to make sure we can learn to fly it. Besides, no one has ever taken a honeymoon to other planets."

"Are you sure you're not ready for a little conventional relaxation on Hawaii?"

"If you insist. It would be fun, but we can go to Hawaii while the ships are being built after we have figured out all the problems. Then we will really need a vacation. It's not like we haven't been living together for three weeks now."

Craig parked the car at the airport. They undressed in the car. They transported to the ship. After making love in zero gee in the star room, the only clothing Dawn found in the ship was a very short red lace negligee top with matching g-string bottom. Craig only found red silk pants. Dawn was ready to travel.

Ship explained the short range transport was like flying an airplane with computer control, "Tell me where you want to go. If you want to fly yourself, then fly me like an airplane. Use the lever on the right to speed up and pull back to slow. Don't worry about crashing into the moon, I am not allowed to permit you to do that. I will automatically slow or just avoid as appropriate."

Craig decided to fly for himself and let Dawn fly until the moon started looming large. Even though they never used much of the potential speed, the trip only took 45 minutes to get close, but then Craig slowed to fly around the moon much slower taking nearly 30 minutes for each orbit and did three orbits before slowing.

Dawn was the first to see something interesting, "Craig, look at that. It looks like the...no; it is the ruins of a city. Look, Craig, there's another smaller city. Craig, look, there's a complete dome."

Craig asked, "Ship, are those cities, and is that really a manmade dome?"

"Yes. I told you that the Atlanteans stopped here on their way from Mars while they waited for their continent to be ready to move onto. Yes, my sensors indicate that the dome you are referring to is intact. However, it has no air. Once the air generation equipment was shut off, it did not take long for the atmosphere of this moon to slip away into space."

Dawn asked, "Is there anyway that we could explore some of the ruins?"

Ship replied, "Yes, Craig could do an invisible teleport to anywhere. He could take you with him that way, but you would have to remain embraced for the trip. Oh, on the third pass I located a village that still has functioning equipment that is still generating an atmosphere inside of its dome. Would you like me to take you there?"

Dawn asked, "Is it representative of the cities, just smaller."

"Yes, except there are no large buildings. I do not know why the original dwellers chose to live outside the main cities, because it is not an agricultural or manufacturing station, just what you would call a suburb or bedroom community for a large city on your Earth. At the height of moon development, the entire planet had enough atmosphere to simulate an altitude of 9,000 feet on Earth. It was enough to moderate the temperature of the whole planet and allow some farming outside the domes. There are always people that want natural food rather than the higher quality manufactured food. As you know, the food I produce cannot be told from the real thing, except my programming does not allow the production of tough beef or fatty hams or over ripe apples. Some people want those substandard things. If you have noticed, my steaks are always well marbled, but without strips of fat and of course it would not make sense to have a bone in the T-bone, but some people want the bone even though they don't eat it. The same with pork chops and baby back rib meat, no wasteful bones. My fruit production is always perfection. I have never understood why some people want less than perfection."

Dawn replied, sounding perturbed, "Ship, just take us to the intact dome with the air inside if it is breathable and of the proper temperature."

"You will find the air good, but the temperature is only 60 degrees. I could teleport clothing first then the two of you."

Craig said, "Do it." They teleported and quickly changed into their clothing. Dawn was provided form fitting jump suit, not tight, but almost like a second skin. Neither of them had seen such material before. The insulation quickly warmed her, but the material was very thin, and yet very strong. It was yellow. Craig's was provided his favorite 501 blue jeans and a yellow jacket. Ship explained the yellow was to help them keep track of each other in case they were separated. Ship could talk directly with Craig, but not with Dawn.

Craig said, "This place looks like it should be inhabited. Because it is sealed and has a positive air pressure, there is no dust on anything. Everything looks perfectly preserved."

Dawn replied, "I know what you mean. I'm almost afraid to go in one of these houses. However, it looks like a European village of the eighteen hundreds." She pushed the pewter (?) handle down on the door and pushed it open. "Look at the furniture. It looks like human furniture, but like nothing I have seen before. It's the right size. The chairs have arms, the seats have cushions, but the cushion is one piece for the whole chair with no seams. Look, there is no seam even on the bottom. It was apparently formed rather than sewn. And...It feels like material on the outside, but it appears to be more of a coating on foam rubber or something. Let's check out their eating and bath rooms."

"Craig, this is an opportunity for Earthmen to make love on another planet. And the moon has only about 1/8 the gravity of the Earth. This may be the only chance anyone has like this for a long time, if ever." They did. As long as they were naked, they decided to zap back up to the ship. As usual on board the ship, the only clothing was provocative. This time Dawn was provided a small skirt. The clothing was really attractive, just skimpy. The village seemed to be only a collection of very identical houses. After returning to the ship, they used the monitors to explore the rest of the village since they had cut their visit short.

When Craig asked Ship about other interesting sites, Ship replied, "The cities were destroyed during meteor showers over the centuries, only a few buildings are still standing. I do not believe there are better specimens than what you saw in the village."

21 MARS

"Craig, let's head for Mars. Ask Ship if there are any good artifacts left there for us to look at."

Ship replied aloud, "Yes, there are the pyramids, the face, and the fortress. Actually, you will find some parts of the fortress that should still be intact, along with the inside areas of the pyramids. Under them were underground cities, but I have no way of knowing the conditions there. I have never been there, I only have records recorded."

"Craig, can I drive?"

"Absolutely, I have only a guess as to which one of those specks are Mars."

Dawn started slow while they could still see their relative speed compared to the Moon and Earth, but as they gradually fell behind she increased speed. "I feel funny about the speed, you can tell Mars is changing, but it is still so far. According to the monitor, ship says that at this speed it will take two days, but look at the speed. We are traveling over 100,000 miles an hour. I know we will be traveling many times that speed, but I am getting tired. Do you see which one is Mars yet?"

"I think so, but why don't we let the ship do the driving?"

"Because I want to make sure that we know how to drive. Don't forget, Ship doesn't know where we are going to find habitable planets. We will have to do the general driving and the other ships don't even have sensors to detect planets at near light speed. Do you realize that means that we will have to find all the planets for the other ships and then provide them the course information for them to take sightings on large constellations to be able to navigate there?"

"No, I had not considered that. Will we have to check on all the ships to make sure they are on course, or will you be able to teach their navigators how to use astral navigation?"

"Some of both, I expect. No. I think that once I have laid out courses, the ships can find them okay. We finding the planets is a big if. Many people don't believe it's possible to have other inhabitable planets because of the probability issue. I won't repeat the formula, but think of it as there being very little probability that a planet will be the right distance from a star of the right kind of light, then having the right minerals, then we have to presume that the DNA forms in the same way or life would be very different from ours."

"I just assumed that things were a little more common. Mars does have ice and an atmosphere similar to ours, but thinner. We have found ice on Titan and other moons. Therefore, if two planets in one solar with ice and the same gases out of only a few, would indicate that there may be many. My concern was running into the people of Atlantis with 10,000 to 50,000 years more history than ours. Actually, worse than that, they were far advanced over us by maybe 100,000 years when they came to Earth. They left this ship behind to rescue Atlanteans that got left behind. What will they think of us if we run into them? Were they Cro-Magnon man that stood upright and taller than the other cavemen and may have had more brain size than ours? Or are we them? Was modern man an Adam and Eve that appeared on Earth similar to the Bible story, but with lots of Adams and lots of Eves? There are a lot of questions. Why don't you put the gas on and let's get to Mars quickly."

"Well, I guess so. It doesn't seem like we are moving even though the speed now says 200,000 miles per hour. Whoa, look at that. We're moving now. Mars is coming up fast now. Look how it's growing in the windshield. Do you still call it a windshield in space with no wind?

"I think viewing port might be more appropriate. What do you think?"

"I think we had better have the ship go into orbit, we're getting close."

Ship replied, "Will enter orbit in three minutes. I will attempt to point out points of interest. A little of my history tells me that before the atmosphere got blown away and the Sun cooled, there was very little ice on the poles. The water did run in the canals. However, water was always at a premium on Mars. Maybe the water shortage was one reason science advanced quickly on Mars. If you note the point on the viewport, we are approaching what was the capitol city with the pyramids, the face and the fort. This was once a very nice park with a lot of green grass and trees. They are gone now. I would recommend some more orbits before deciding where to explore next."

"And I would recommend that we eat and sleep."

Craig said, "I agree." They reviewed their plans for the next few years and their visit to the Moon as they ate. Dawn went to sleep with her head in Craig's lap. He carried her into the four poster bed and they slept for a solid 10 hours. In the morning they viewed recordings of the surface on the big screen television in the lounge or living room that the ship had made while they slept. All of the shots were from space, but with very close zoom shots.

Ship narrated for them, "If you watch the window in the corner it will show the distance shot that will give you the location of the artifact in relation to the surface of Mars. The main screen will be the zoom in views." Zooming in on the pyramids showed the intricate stone work that built them. The lines were not visible in all places due to the disintegration of the stones over the millennium. The same was true of the fortress and the face. In fact, the lines on the foot were completely filled in with powder or something to the point that lines between stones only showed from inches away on zoom. "The face was carved from a solid block of stone from the core of the mountain. The fortress and pyramids were also based upon an original carving out of the mountain. Stones were only used to fill in spaces and for repairs over the years as the storms on Mars became greater with the cooling of the sun. Both the pyramids and the fortress have tunnels and manmade rooms inside. The tallest pyramid used to hold the history of what you call the Atlanteans, but it is empty now. There are a few insignificant artifacts in both the pyramids and the fortress. However, the best artifacts are located in an underground vault that was used as a command post for the last people on Mars. I would highly recommend it. The system is generating a breathable atmosphere. However, there is a very cool temperature of 44 degrees Fahrenheit there. Craig will have to go by himself on this one."

Dawn said, "That's not fair. We'll just have to figure out how we are going to do this. It's not that cold there. Craig, you can't catch a cold. How did I know that? Anyway, Ship, just send the warm clothing first and then we'll go down." They undressed each other slowly and then hugged and zapped down.

They found themselves in a large control room with apparently live pictures from around Mars. Thankfully, Dawn was provided with what appeared to be a ski outfit with long warm solid neon blue pants, matching jacket and white boots. It would have been attractive anywhere. It was could have been a modern control room from Earth. It looked normal except that again there were no seams on the cushions. There were various chairs positioned around, attached to the floor facing different screens. There was a control console in the middle that one had to stand to use.

Craig said, "Ship says to press the green arrow pointing to the right."

Dawn said, "I hope it doesn't start some kind of self destruct mechanism. They could not understand the words at first.

Unasked for, Ship teleported down a speaker box so that Dawn and Craig could both hear a translation into English since no current Earthman had ever seen, let alone heard Atlantean, let alone this ancient version from 60,000 years ago. Craig could have had the translation by telepathy from the ship, but Ship wanted them both to hear the words simultaneously. Ship computed to itself, "I am very impressed with this Dawn and other women that Craig has met. I was programmed that only men could be Captain, maybe my programming was incomplete." Ship said aloud over the speaker box, "Craig, Dawn, I will translate for you. Turn the black knob counterclockwise to where you can barely hear it and then I will provide a translation. I have to hear the speaker to translate, because this is not programmed into my memory bank."

The translation was louder than the control room speakers and had no noticeable delay in translation. "Welcome. You may or may not be descendants of the people that produced this historical document, but you will find this interesting and informative. It may help your civilization. What you are seeing now is some historical footage taken three hundred years before we left the planet. The planet was not red from space when these pictures were taken, but green and blue. There were mighty seas, rivers and canals that provided for all of our heavy traffic. Our private travel was by roads to and from the farms and by air for between cities and villages. Within town we used automobiles for transportation. These were owned by the town or city and available for anyone's use at any time. If there was not one in sight, the person could press a button near all of the exterior doors in town and a vehicle would be there within two minutes. While traveling, the vehicle would be as if you owned it, but when you excited the vehicle for more than two minutes, it would take any call directed to it by the central computer. All of the vehicles, aircraft, ships, farm trucks, home lighting, communications, and all else operates with electricity that is broadcast world wide for everyone's use. We started using orbital relay stations 10 centuries ago rather than use local power generation. Dawn would you press the square red button next to the green arrow you pressed before.

Thank you. I wanted to stop the history lesson to explain a little. The 10 centuries was actually given by number of revolutions around the Sun but computed by me to Earth time to help you understand. The power generation stations were the pyramids that I pointed out earlier. Apparently, there is little correlation between these pyramids and the ones on Earth or something is missing from my programming. At any rate, power was generated in the pyramids converted to beamed energy and transmitted to an overhead constellation of satellites like your communications and the Global Positioning System (GPS) satellites of Earth. Just as many of Earth's satellites are used by whoever has the money, these were available to all with no money exchanged, but provided as part of the world government. The satellites then retransmitted the power to rooftop antennas or to vehicle antennas to power their electric motors. This meant that they did not need to have heavy batteries or fuel of any kind on board. The only non-cargo weight was the aircraft of the vehicle itself and the electric motors. All of the aircraft used propellers with ducted thrust design, at this time. Okay, Dawn, if you are ready to go on, press the green arrow again."

Dawn asked, "Was this beamed energy electricity as we know it?"

"No, it was more like a particle beam. The particles were taken from the planet and beamed at the satellites that then used the incoming matter to store and retransmit. It is similar to how I used matter to store and then use energy for power. However, I was built 50,000 years later and can teleport my own power to use for energy. Teleportation was unknown on Mars. Note that they never use the word Mars, they never had a name other than the generic 'our planet'." Dawn pressed the green button.

The translation continued, "Notice the green. The temperature was maintained relatively constant world wide and there was no permanent ice. Every imaginable edible plant was abundant. The daily..."

Dawn whispered to Craig not listening to the daily life portion of the translation, "Craig, look at their clothing. No one is wearing a top and everyone wears only a skirt type cloth that only comes to mid thigh. No wonder ship skimps on the clothing. I'm lucky to have a top on board the ship. Their cars are absolutely box like. They look like the tram around the Dallas Fort Worth Airport, except that people are driving them. Can you imagine no one owning them? I wonder if anyone owns anything."

Craig said, "Maybe they'll tell us if we listen." Dawn frowned at him, but rather than pout decided he was right, they should listen instead of talk. Next time, she would just stop the recording when she wanted to talk.

"Yes, Dawn, people did own their houses and private possessions, but transportation was public. Now we are flying over the fields to the next city and if you will notice, Dawn, their airships look like B-2 bombers except with ducted thrust. The fields are green and lush as far as the eye can see. I hope you don't mind if I interject a few explanations as we go." Ship was now going beyond translation.

The pictures on their surround screens changed abruptly to red blowing dust. The city they arrived at had a dome. Ship's translation continued, "You may not have realized, but our ship is now passing over those very same fields toward the very same town, but 300 years later. You can see that fields have dried up and the town now sports a dome to keep out the dust and concentrate the air. The Sun has developed sun spots and solar flares that are impacting our climate dramatically world wide. Not all areas are this bad, but mankind is retreating from the poles toward the equator which now has a better climate. The sun spots are caused by burnt out nuclear fuel that has been fusioned and fissioned so many times that it creates a crust on the Sun. As a result internal pressure on the sun flares out elsewhere interrupting our communications and power broadcasts. The atmosphere is being blown away by solar gusts from the Sun and as it does, the towns must pump in huge quantities of atmosphere to keep the air pressure up to comfortable levels. The crops in this area of the planet have died out and food is being manufactured in newly developed matter converters. The people here collect ordinary dirt, input it into nuclear fusion/fission devices and reconstitute the minerals as food. The quality is poor compared to naturally grown food, but nutritious."

Craig said, "Well, I'm tired. What about you Dawn? Ready to go back to the ship?"

"No, let's look at their living quarters here before we go back." Dawn took off down a hallway and turned in the first door. "This must have been their eating facility."

"It looks pretty ordinary for a Mars eating facility. There is the food synthesizer and a table and some chairs. Ten chairs to be exact. If this is an eating room, the crew of this facility was very small."

Dawn had gone across the hall and opened another door. "Craig! Look here. This must have been a library. There is a television and here are some crystal cubes that must be like our CD recordings. Maybe there are movies here that will tell us more about them. And there are books here. They have pictures and some strange characters that must be their alphabet. Maybe scientists on Earth can use the combination to understand their language."

"Actually ship understands their language just fine. However, I'll have ship take these back with us when we go. I think we found whatever we are going to find here. The planet sacrificed to save its young reproductive people. I don't think we are going to find anything exciting here. This place is military plain with gray walls and plain sleeping quarters. I suggest that we get back to the ship for some sleep." They did.

"Dawn, good morning. What are we going to do today?"

"Let's go home."

"I agree, Dawn. If this was the center of their civilization there is nothing for us there. We were hundreds of years too late, but we now have some form of recordings from their library to learn from." Craig and

Dawn told Ship to take them back to Earth and watched recorded movies then went to bed depressed.

Right before going to sleep, Dawn told Craig, "On Earth, the people survived even after Atlantis was destroyed, but here Mars was not friendly enough for them to survive.

"We were supposed to be 100 years ahead of where we are. I wonder why the Atlanteans did not come back to make sure their Martian ancestors were dead before going off into space."

"I don't know. Ship should have us back home when we wake up."

When they woke, they could see Earth through the window. They were back in orbit. As they ate pancakes and sausage for breakfast Craig said, "How far are we from getting mankind into space?"

Dawn replied, "We can't get mankind into space. At most a few." She thought, "I am talking serious. I guess people that live on a deserted island would get used to wearing nothing."

"How many people are there? Seven billion? How many ships would it take? How many ships could be built? At the rate we are going it would take a year just to get the basic technology in place for a second rate ship. The nearly instantaneous capabilities of Ship were far beyond what he could hope for. The best engines they could hope for Earth to produce would take months to accelerate to light speed. I created a ten thousand fold breakthrough in computer technology, but there will only be a small piece of data on each ship compared to this ship. Maximum production of the new computer is max'd out at 40 per month. We have less than nine years left so that means there will only be about 4000 ships of roughly 1000 people, or 4 million that we can save."

Dawn interrupted, "And they will be flying blind. We will have to do the exploring for them so I can give them the astral navigation to their new homes."

Craig said, "Who do we save? Americans? A few from each area of the world? The Red Chinese? Who?"

Dawn said, "I honestly don't know, Craig, but we have nine more years to figure that out, explore near star systems, train crews, and that assumes that we can get everyone to work toward the same goals. Will Congress fund the effort if they can't leave with their own families or at least get their kids into space?"

.

22 EXPLORATIONS

When they got back to Earth they both got involved in their work. Dawn was teaching her classes in navigation between the stars and Craig was working on mass production of food stuffs and ships. Five months later, Dawn's classes as a PhD instructor finished for the semester.

"Craig, I think we need a vacation. Want to go planet searching?"

"Why not? There is nothing for me to do really. Congress has appropriated all the money we need. Scientists and engineers are working toward space with minimal pay. They have the processes worked out for building the ships. Due to the aerodynamics and light weight, they can easily boost the ships into space when the time comes. The nuclear fusion propulsion engines have been tested. They are pretty inefficient compared to the goals, but we have years to continue development. The biggest problem facing us is manufacturing the ships, but there is nothing for me to do."

"Let's make a show of going off to the South Pacific on some of your lottery winnings and taking a long vacation. We can then be absent for weeks without suspicion."

"Sounds good to me. I'll call a meeting between the heads of research to tell them they will be on their own for awhile."

"We had both better be thinking about things we can do to entertain ourselves on the trip."

"I can think of only one thing the ship can't provide."

"Oh, Silly. I mean like making a list of movies we haven't seen or would like to see again. Music that we haven't had time for these past months." We can go through some of the history of Mars we took from the library on Mars.

Three days later, they zapped to the Ship for a long trip. They had gotten used to running around on the ship half naked and had been living together for nearly a year now.

Craig said, "Any particular aiming point?"

"Let's head toward Orion. I think maybe that is where the Atlanteans went."

"Right, they built pyramids on both Earth and Mars in the pattern of Orion's belt. Sounds as good as any. What if we find them?"

"Let's worry about that when we find them. Remember, 10,000 years ago, they left this ship for us. They must be good."

"Ship, you heard her, but before we go, refresh us on how we find planets at infinite speed."

"I can do it for you. I keep track of everything within several million miles of the ship and everything moon size within hundred million miles of our course. If I spot an object big enough to have natural gravity and near enough to a star for heat, then I look closer at the object. I can use spectral analysis of any atmosphere to detect oxygen, nitrogen, any harmful gases, or beneficial gases. I check for the presence of water. I then detect any life factors, like chlorophyll in plants or moving warm blooded creatures.

Temperature is of course critical. If these tests are passed, I will notify you of my findings and you can tell me to look closer. I can detect electrical emissions of an advanced civilization from even further off than I can other life signs. If you like I will tell you of any emissions as soon as detected."

"Sounds good to me. Let us know of anything that could be civilization or anything Earthlike. We can then have you deviate from course to head in that direction. Dawn, give the go ahead."

"Thank you Craig. In fact, I think I would like to start out at the controls before we let the ship take over."

"Okay, I'll sit with you. It might be interesting to watch the acceleration."

They sat at the console in front of the clear view screen in the control room and Dawn pushed the throttle forward. The moon was left behind quickly. "Dawn, look at the rearward monitor, it's your last glimpse of Earth and the Moon for awhile. See them getting smaller, and smaller, and now they look like marbles. Now they are gone."

"Thanks for pointing that out. That was neat. Almost sad though. One day before long, it will be forever. Eventually we will never see Earth again. It will be a memory and eventually forgotten. Do you think the Atlanteans have forgotten Earth?"

"I think I have miscalculated the asteroid."

"What!" Craig exclaimed.

Ship expounded upon the interruption," *The asteroid storm is less than two years away from Earth."*

"Two years! I thought we had more than nine years left. Are you sure there is an asteroid? How can you have it wrong by eight years?"

"I have been sitting in orbit for twenty thousand years until you started this trip to the stars. Therefore, I have not been keeping track of objects in space. Apparently when

the last Atlanteans left me fifteen thousand years ago, they miscalculated by years, which is not very much in relation to the time they left me."

"So explain what this trip did."

"I was going to. My long range sensors have not been used in ten thousand years. As you had me setting out to travel between stars my programming caused me to turn on the long range sensors and start testing the range. Normally, I do not detect such small objects at long range, but we are headed toward the object and I since I knew the calculated course, I decided to search for it just as a test of my systems. I found it, but it was too close. People from Earth could see it with their telescopes within the next few months if they knew where to look. It is not an asteroid from the asteroid belt, but a moon type object that was knocked free from some ancient planet millennium ago. It is four hundred miles across and will intersect at the current Earth orbit in April, two years from now. It appears to be a solid object like iron ore."

"Do you mean April, less than two years from now?"

"Yes,"

"Craig, we had better head back now and tell them them the bad news."

"Ship, you heard her. We have a lot of work to do. Take control and as soon as we get close enough zap us back to our apartment and then go into orbit to await further instruction."

23 CHANGED EXPECTATIONS

Dawn said, "There is too much for the two of us to do. We need more help. Are you sure the ship cannot take on a larger crew? There is plenty of room for a few more."

"I agree that we could use more help, but Ship said that I could only bring a wife on board with me. No one else. Isn't that right, Ship?"

"Actually, I said wives on board. There are seven chairs at the dining room table. The people of Atlantis had many wives. There is only one captain and only one captain's chair, but there are six side chairs. You and Dawn have already come to the conclusion that women make better space travelers. It is also important to have more women to build the population when colonizing new worlds."

Dawn broke the ensuing silence, "Craig. We did come to that conclusion ourselves. We just did not apply it to ourselves. What is our personal mission besides advancing science?"

"We have to find planets for the colony or colonies."

"Then we need a zoologist, a botanist, a geologist to tell us about minerals available, and an archeologist if we keep coming across the remains of Atlantis, and what?"

"An outdoorsman, er a woman. Someone that can lead an expedition on a strange planet. A survivalist type.

"Didn't you tell me you had researched other women before choosing me? I think you better see who is available."

"But we are married and I can't marry more than one nor do I want to."

"Craig, legal marriage is an Earth law. Ship has its own definition. If I remember, you chose me out of necessity. Well, this is necessary too. You don't really have a choice. We have to accelerate progress, find new planets to go to. You told me how you were attracted to some of the other women and chose me because I had a unique background is astral navigation which was critical. You married me because I wanted to be married if we were going to live together for the years to prepare. Well, things change. Now you need quantity not a single choice."

VOLUME II

Coming Soon

The story continues in volume II. Craig increases his crew on Ship by adding those girls he previously met before his official marriage to Dawn. Together they develop selection processes and training classes for the crews of the evacuation fleets and work with other countries to build and select their crews.

Ship is used with its full crew to search the Milky Way Galaxy for other

Earthlike planets, finding several. One planet was prepared to receive evacuees by the Atlanteans as they headed out to the stars. Other planets are found with agreeable ecosystems conducive to human life with good atmosphere, safe plant life, very much Earthlike except for the lack of humans. Some are found that appear excellent but are inhabited by dangerous creatures.

The meager fleets leave Earth and journey to the stars to continue human life as Earth, as we know it, is destroyed.

The crew of Ship discovers a benefit of being the crew. Ship transports its crew by disintegrating the human body and reassembling its molecular structure based on their genetics and in the process healing any weaknesses or injuries during the transport process. Whereas they may have initially had previous injuries and scars, those are healed during the first transport. As a result, every time they transport to or from Ship they are returned to the age they were during that initial transport. While they continue learning from experience and ship, their bodies are no longer aging. The brain shrinkage that occurs with age does not exist for the Ship's crew.

ABOUT THE AUTHOR

The Author spent over 39 years with the United States Air Force in the USA, Asia, and Europe. He had some part in the development of most of the new weapons system in development between 1979 and 1989. Some of those systems are just now being delivered. He taught classes in weapons system research and development and logistics management as a guest lecturer at the Air Force Institute of Technology and various conference rooms around the USA. Over 3000 current and future managers attended his class on R&D scheduling. He served on many brain storming teams to come up with unique solutions to military problems from shooting down space objects to moving "dud" bombs off an active runway.

He is now retired from both active duty and civil service. He is still active in writing, the local amateur radio club, towing the Shriner float in parades and going to almost weekly dances and generally enjoying himself.

www.ingramcontent.com/pod-product-compliance
Lightning Source LLC
LaVergne TN
LVHW061544070526
838199LV00077B/6889
* 9 7 9 8 8 6 9 1 2 9 0 9 3 *